White Shadow

Godmother to a Revolution

By Libby James

Library of Congress Control Number: 2017956170
ISBN-10: 0996881921
ISBN-13: 978-0-9968819-2-0

Penstemon
Publications
Wellington, Colorado

Introduction

Mozambique is a young country, existing as an independent nation only since 1975. Its history, so raw and so recent, is incomplete without the story of Janet Rae Johnson Mondlane, an American who played a major role in Mozambique's fight for freedom from 500 years of Portuguese domination. Dubbed "Godmother to a Revolution" by journalist Robin Wright, the details of her life and work are revealed through 7,000 letters exchanged between Janet and Eduardo Mondlane.

Janet lost her heart to Eduardo when she was seventeen and never wavered in her devotion to this man who led a revolution that lasted for a decade. She became his advisor, organizer, and founder of the Mozambique Institute that provided educational and health services for the freedom fighters. There were times when only her encouragement and insistence kept him from abandoning such an enormous and dangerous task.

White Shadow is a novel based on her extraordinary life and would not have been possible without access to the work of Nadja Manghezi who compiled the Mondlane letters in *An African Has My Heart In His Hand*.

Dedication

To Kristin, Kurt, Jeff and Jeni and their dozen offspring.

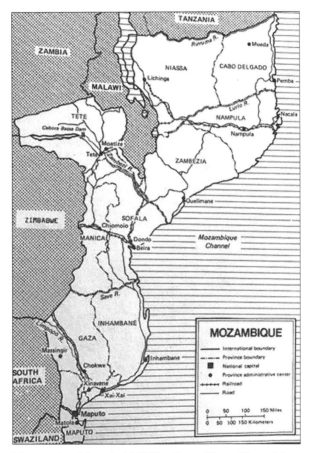

Map reproduced from *And Still They Dance, Women War and the Struggle for Change in Mozambique* by Stephanie Urdang

A portion of proceeds from the sale of *White Shadow* will go to support the Eduardo Mondlane Foundation.

Table of Contents

Table of Contents

Chapter 1
The Spell is Cast

Janet Rae Johnson helped herself to a seat, front row center. A stream of young people trickled in to the high-ceilinged auditorium with a glass wall overlooking Lake Geneva at a Christian church camp in Wisconsin. She wasn't a sit-in-the-front-row kind of person but today she was on a mission, determined to catch every word. The speaker was from Africa. Ever since she had traced the course of the Limpopo River with her finger on the globe in her fourth grade geography class, Africa had been vivid in Janet's imagination. So strange, so far away. So different from her life in Indianapolis, Indiana.

He took the stage. Eduardo Chivambo Mondlane, a tall very-black black man wearing a crisp, white short-sleeved shirt with an open collar, brilliant against his skin, and a pair of sharply creased khaki pants. He smiled, waved and the lively teens quieted. This man who looked so different from these teens and whose gaze seemed to penetrate--to demand their attention--had them curious enough to quit squirming in their chairs, poking at each other and calling out to their friends.

Eduardo had cast a spell. Especially upon Janet. She could not keep her eyes off him or listen intently enough. She needed to absorb every word. Perhaps it was his sleek, muscular body and those eyes, so deep and dark, so animated. And that springy head of hair, close cropped and glistening. Or was it his words, the energy that flowed from him, his goals and his vision of an independent future for his country?

Janet wanted to bounce her fingers off his hair and feel the smoothness of his dark-chocolate skin. Transfixed by his booming, melodic voice, she leaned forward as he spoke about his homeland, mired for

1

so long under the harsh colonial thumb of Portugal. He described his determination to seek independence from Portuguese rule for the people of Mozambique. He wasn't at all sure just how he would accomplish it, but he had a clear vision of what he wanted to do.

Church camp lasted for two weeks. The idea was to attend a talk on a different topic each day, but Janet chose to attend Eduardo's talk every day of the week he spent at camp. Every day she learned more about this 31-year-old man from a small village in the bush of sub-Saharan Africa on an incredibly long and difficult journey to obtain his education. She realized from listening to his words that nothing was going to stop him.

It was one thing for Janet to see him and hear him, but now she wanted him to see her. Yet how? The camp was large and every time she spotted him, he was hurrying somewhere or deep in conversation, surrounded by several campers. She hatched a plan. She'd write an article for the camp newspaper about his talks and then hunt him down to give his approval for her words. She wrote the piece, then found him strolling away from the showers near the camp's volleyball court, hair still wet and dripping. She hurried toward him, waving her paper.

"My name's Janet and I've written a piece for the camp newspaper about your talks. Would you mind checking it over?"

"Be happy to." He smiled at her and ran a hand through his hair, shaking off silvery drops of water. He took the paper and settled himself on the ground at the edge of the grassy playing field. Janet flung her long brown hair over her shoulder and plunked down beside him. She hoped she looked appealing in her light-green sleeveless shirt with a wispy little scarf tied round her neck to match the deep green of her Bermuda shorts. She liked her looks best in summer when her skin was lightly tanned and complemented her green-flecked eyes. This morning she'd made sure to shave her legs and paint the toenails that poked out from her leather sandals a brilliant red.

Eduardo took his time reading, nodding, a smile crossing his face now and then. "How old are you?" He shot her a questioning look.

"Seventeen." She had an odd hope that he'd think seventeen old enough. For what, she wasn't sure, but at least old enough to hold his attention.

2

"Really. I don't know anyone your age who writes like this."

She silently congratulated herself. She knew her writing was strong. She began to think that her words had made him take notice, maybe even persuaded him that she was intelligent and mature for her age.

Eduardo handed the article back to her but seemed in no hurry to leave. As the late afternoon sun sank toward the horizon, the two of them fell into step, meandering side-by-side across the playing field toward the lake. It seemed to Janet that their talk flowed effortlessly. In some eerie way, she felt as if they'd known each other in another time. She was overcome with a crazy sense that somehow she was drawing this mysterious dark man toward her.

She moved through the next few days in a pleasant semi-daze, making no effort to hide the smile that seemed permanently plastered to her face.

* * * * *

A nearly full moon shone liquid splashes of light onto the rippling waters of Lake Geneva. Embers from a giant dying campfire on the beach added a red-orange glow to the night as campers began to wander away from their final gathering. It was Friday night and church camp was coming to an end. Over the days, friendships had flourished. Parting was going to be bittersweet.

Without asking, Eduardo took Janet's hand in his and drew her away from the campfire, leading her down the sandy beach. It was ridiculous, really. After all, he was thirty-one, a man on a mission--yet here he was, actually contemplating a step fraught with danger for reasons way more serious than their difference in age and the responsibility he felt to complete his education and one day serve his country. Not allowing himself to ponder this thought for the moment, he took her small, pale hand and led her toward an ancient vine-covered gazebo out of sight of the campers and the dwindling fire.

Janet welcomed the sweaty warmth of his palm and the surprising tingle that zinged through her body as he squeezed her hand tight. At the gazebo, he paused for a moment and then, with a moment of hesitation, made a gesture toward pressing his lips against hers. He had

3

barely brushed against her face when she pulled back and turned her head away.

More than anything, she wanted this man to kiss her, but something insistent in her gut warned her, no, not now. If she really wanted to entice this man into loving her, and she knew without question that she did, she sensed that she would need the cunning to play her hand with care. It had been less than a week, but she knew that this encounter was no teenage summer fling. This was for keeps. And nothing was going to stop her from pursuing this man.

Eduardo didn't force the kissing issue. He backed away, just a little, then gently circled his arms around her shoulders and guided her toward a rough wooden bench. Huddled close to each other, bathed by the moonlight, they stayed there in the seclusion of the gazebo, holding each other and talking, at times just being quiet, losing all track of time. Way too quickly, Janet thought, the sky began to lighten and the dawn rose muggy-hot and oppressive.

They left the gazebo and hand-in-hand made their way down the beach and through the wet grass toward Janet's cabin. Eduardo squeezed her hand and smiled into her eyes as they parted. He promised to come by later to say goodbye. Sarah, Janet's cabin mate, who happened to be one of the few black girls at camp, was sound asleep when Janet slipped noiselessly into her bunk bed.

* * * * *

A few hours later on that misty Saturday morning, Eduardo tapped on Janet's cabin door. "Hi. You in there?"

"Just a minute." Janet tossed a pile of shirts and shorts into a suitcase and opened the door. "Come in." She grabbed her little box Brownie camera. "Can I take your picture? Stand right there with Sarah." Sarah stood still and stared. Eduardo smiled. Janet snapped. Then Janet asked Sarah to take a picture of her with Eduardo.

"Can I write to you?" She gave him a pleading little look and tucked a slip of paper with her address on it into his hand.

"Is there any way I can stop you?" With only a slight hint of a smile, he scribbled a few lines on a scrap of paper and placed it into her hand with a squeeze. Then he was gone.

4

Chapter 2
Back Home in Indiana

❝Where did you meet the black girl?" Back home in Indianapolis, Janet showed her parents photos from church camp. "I don't understand," her mother said. Her dad said nothing.

Janet felt a twinge in her stomach. "But Mom, you've always--."

"Were there many black children at camp?"

"Her name is Sarah. She was my cabin mate. There were only a few black campers, and they stayed mostly to themselves." She put her fingers on her stomach, all of a sudden slightly queasy.

"I'm surprised. That's all." Winifred ran her fingers through her curly brown hair, slightly streaked with gray, then smoothed her flowered cotton skirt over her knees.

Janet glanced outside at the tidy green lawn, at the neatly clipped edges and her young brother Chuck's bicycle leaning against the leafy maple that shaded the living room. "Sarah seemed a sad girl, didn't have much to say to me or to anyone really. By the time we crawled into our bunks at night, we were both too tired to talk. We didn't get to know each other very well."

"I didn't know black kids went to camp." Winifred frowned. "How did she happen to share a cabin with you?"

"Before I went to camp, I checked "yes" on a form saying I wouldn't mind sharing a cabin with a black girl. I guess that's how. It worked out fine."

"Interesting. Why would you do that? What were you thinking?"

Janet didn't answer. Instead she turned the conversation to all she'd learned at camp about Africa, especially about Portuguese East Africa, the country that would one day become Mozambique. Portugal had been sucking their colony dry and contributing practically noth-

5

ing to its welfare off and on for 500 years. She pointed to the photo of Eduardo. "This man from Mozambique shared his vision with us. He plans to make his country an independent nation. He's in the U.S. to complete his education. I wrote about the talks he gave for the camp newspaper." She showed her parents the article. "I'm pretty proud of this. Want to read it?"

"When I have some time, I will," her mother said.

She walked away and began dusting the living room furniture with great vigor. Janet's dad, Raymond, ensconced in his favorite chair, pushed his glasses up on his nose, put his feet up and without a word returned to the book he'd been reading.

Janet's stomach cramped, deeper and stronger. How would her parents feel if they learned about her fascination, and yes, attraction, to this black man? Why had she assumed that they would think nothing of it? That they would both be interested in knowing all about this incredible man. Suddenly her world seemed a little off kilter and confusing. Things didn't seem quite right or true. Her parents had always been good listeners, anxious to hear about her enthusiasms. Why weren't they now? She wondered. But one thing she knew for certain-- the power of the feelings she held deep inside for Eduardo.

*****

For fifteen months, Janet and Eduardo did not see each other, or even speak. Phone calls were way too expensive.

Janet knew that Eduardo was spending the weeks before his classes began at Oberlin College touring the Midwest sharing his story at churches and summer camps. He had agreed to give these presentations when he was granted a scholarship to complete his undergraduate degree in sociology. Begun first in South Africa, his college studies had dragged on for years, interrupted when he was labeled an "unwanted foreigner" and forced to leave South Africa when the apartheid laws went into effect. He was thwarted again as he attempted to resume his studies in Portugal, hassled by government officials. His reputation for activism had followed him across the ocean.

*****

A letter from Eduardo arrived a few days after Janet was home.

6

She devoured every squiggle on the page and wrote back the very same day. That was the day when she began living for his letters. The exchange soon grew intense. Eduardo didn't hold back. "I might be wrong to say I love you, but love can't be controlled. It cares not for the years between our ages or the difference in the colors of our skin."

Janet clung to every word. "There is no yes or no to my love for you. It just is," she replied.

It felt good to be back at Broad Ripple High School for her senior year. Immersing herself in her studies gave Janet a sense of fulfillment. But it was Eduardo who dominated her thoughts. She was desperate to see him again. She dreamed up a scheme to make that happen. She would invite him to give a talk at her church. He could stay at her house for the weekend.

Her dad was reading in his favorite chair in the living room when he overheard Janet. "Do you think he'd come?" Janet was telling a friend who had been at camp with her about her plan. Her friend knew about Janet's interest in Eduardo and understood how badly she wanted to see him again.

"Great idea. That would give you at least a couple of days together."

Janet's dad, the mild-mannered Raymond—a man of few words who spent most of his free time deep in a book or newspaper—shouted out.

"Wait just a minute there, Janet. There's something you need to know. What's his name? Eduardo? No. He cannot stay in this house."

"But why not?"

Winifred appeared from the kitchen. "Because your father and I say so."

"We are aware that you admire this man. I'm sure he is a great speaker, but sorry, he cannot stay here--not ever." Raymond got up from his chair. He was working hard to keep his voice steady.

"But why?" Janet asked again.

She'd been taken off guard by her parents' explosive reaction. "Is it because he's black?"

No answer.

"That must be why. The church says all men are created equal under God. I've been told that since I was small. Do you believe what the church says?"

"We do." Winifred picked up where Raymond left off. "Equal, but not the same. We're treading on forbidden ground here. You may not invite him to stay at our house."

"I don't understand why the color of his skin matters so much to you. He's a brilliant man with a world-changing mission." Janet knew her parents took their religion seriously. They'd met in a Methodist Youth group, were faithful churchgoers and Bible readers, and saw to it that their children were as well. They had encouraged her attendance at church camp ever since she'd been old enough to leave home overnight. She liked going to camp and that pleased her parents—until now.

Her family wasn't the kind who mulled over controversial issues of the day around the dinner table with their children. Talk stuck pretty much to local events—things like how school was going and music lessons. It was obvious to Janet that her parents had a strong sense of right and wrong, but it wasn't until she showed an interest in Eduardo that she began to learn how they felt about black people. Did they think their children would figure these things out for themselves without being told? Janet went to school with nearly all white kids. She'd never had a black friend. The question of inviting one into her home had never come up.

As she pondered her parents' outburst, she thought back to a time when her mother had discouraged her friendship with a schoolmate, Harriet Friedlander. She had told Janet not to invite Harriet into their home. "She's Jewish." Her mother said no more, as if that were explanation enough.

Janet caught on fast. Now she knew that it would not be wise for her parents to see the flow of letters that were flying between her and Eduardo. She was surprised that they had not discovered them already. It was probably because she was usually first to check the mailbox every day, anxious to see what it might contain. She began scheming to conceal the arrival of Eduardo's letters by making sure she was always first at the mailbox.

Every night after dinner she disappeared to her room to do her homework. She didn't allow herself to take Eduardo's photo from her dresser drawer until she had finished her studies. Then she sat on her bed staring at it, thinking happy thoughts about him before she began to pour out her feelings onto the page. She wrote with abandon. Mornings on her way to school, she slipped her latest letter into a neighborhood mailbox.

Once, out shopping with her mother, Janet carelessly left one of Eduardo's letters on the seat of the car while she ran into the post office to buy stamps. While Winifred waited, she saw the letter and idly picked it up. She began to read. "What in the world is going on between you and this man?" Winifred was fuming by the time Janet returned to the car. "How can you possibly have romantic feelings for this--this person? For your own good, you must end this relationship now." She thrust the letter at her daughter's chest.

Janet didn't answer. She swallowed hard, squeezed her fists and toes together and blinked her eyes to forestall the tears. Inside she was boiling, but she forced herself to bring her feelings down to a controllable simmer. She sensed that whatever she said in reply would only make her mother even angrier than she was. So she managed to say nothing, for the first time in her life using a strategy she would turn to often. When an encounter became too hot, too uncomfortable, she simply stopped speaking. Even among her closest friends, when conflict threatened, she shut down. They rode home in silence.

Janet had always been her father's good girl, the serious student who brought home 'A' studded report cards. She was so different from Delores, her artistic older sister who struggled so with academics. Her brother Chuck, still in elementary school, was pretty much an unknown quantity. Janet felt close to her father and on some vague subliminal level sensed that he pinned high hopes on her.

As she grew older, her persistent dream of somehow getting involved in Africa had seemed a good fit with her father's wishes for her. He wanted his precocious daughter to become a doctor and then perhaps a medical missionary, and he had told her so.

The letters Janet wrote to Eduardo increasingly became her emotional escape valve. In them she laid out the jumble of her feelings unedited, in an attempt to sort them out for herself. She needed to find a way to ease the frustration she felt around her feelings for Eduardo and the opinions of her parents. He became the sounding board for the tangled thoughts running around in her head that she could not share with anyone else.

"I believe marriage is the ultimate expression of one's love for another but I can see that sometimes marriages go stale," she wrote to Eduardo. "I watch my mother keep house, go to club meetings and shop. My father goes to work, to church, to events at the Masonic Lodge. That's all there is in their lives. That's not enough for me. I want to contribute to the welfare of mankind and I can't do it by 'settling down.' My mother says I'm an idealist and that I'll outgrow these thoughts, but I won't. If I married you, I could help to improve the lot of your people. I could sustain you in your time of need and share in your work."

*****

Months went by. In May 1952 Janet graduated from high school with honors. In the fall she enrolled as a pre-med student at Miami University in Oxford, Ohio. Soon she was struggling through chemistry class and beginning to wonder if pursuing a degree in medicine was the right choice for her. The letters between Janet and Eduardo continued to flow. It was more than a year since they'd seen each other. One day Eduardo wrote saying he'd been asked to speak at a Christian Youth Conference at Ohio University in Athens, 200 miles across the state from where Janet was in school.

Eduardo did not ask that she meet him in Athens, but Janet was no dummy. She saw an opportunity and was quick to seize it. She was certain that her parents would give their permission for her to attend a Christian conference. A college girl needed her parents' blessing before she could leave campus overnight, after all.

She took a bus to Athens, carrying with her a chemistry book and a small overnight bag slung over the shoulder of her yellow crew neck sweater complemented by a black and yellow plaid skirt, saddle shoes and white socks. She tried her best to study as the bus wound around the rolling countryside alight with the reds, oranges and yellows of fall leaves fluttering from the trees. She didn't have much luck with the studying though. Her single, overpowering goal was to be with Eduardo and she could not think about anything else.

Eduardo hitched a ride to Athens with Roger, a classmate and seminary student from Alabama, anxious to attend the conference for all the right reasons. Roger seemed surprised at how quiet the normally chatty Eduardo was during the trip. Perhaps he was concentrating on the talks he was scheduled to give.

Janet shuffled through great mounds of crunchy leaves as she walked from the bus stop to the campus. She dropped her bag at the dorm room she'd been assigned and hurried to the auditorium just in time to see Eduardo approach the stage. She slipped silently into the only remaining seat in the front row, folded her hands across her knees and took a deep breath.

As he began to speak, she noticed that his hair had grown longer and if anything, his eyes were more alluring, more dynamic, than she remembered. A shiver ran through her whole body when he began to speak in the booming voice she hadn't heard for so many months. Her skin tingled. It felt surreal to be so close to him. She'd held his image in her heart for so long. Now that he was in front of her smiling, gesturing, his deep voice explaining the upheavals underway in Africa, she was captivated all over again.

When he finished speaking, Eduardo took questions from the audience. Endless questions, it seemed to Janet. Finally he finished up and thanked the audience for their interest. Then he was free to move toward her, eyes smiling deeply into hers, big sturdy hand reaching out to pull her toward him for a hug, unaware of or just not caring who might be watching. "It's been a while." He looked into her eyes. "Too long. Way too long."

"I know you so much better now." She clasped his hand and smiled up at him. "Thank God for your letters. They have been my life line."

When they stood side-by-side waiting in line for a cafeteria lunch a few minutes later, Eduardo introduced Janet to Danielle Nelson,

11

president of a national Methodist women's group. "We became friends at Lake Geneva camp two summers ago." Then he picked up a tray warily eyeing the bright green squares of Jell-O shimmering before him. He didn't take any.

"Oh, hello." Danielle mumbled the words, glancing at Janet for a moment, then looking away as she reached for a steaming bowl of macaroni and cheese. Her attention returned to Eduardo. "You have such a way with words, Eduardo. I can hardly wait to hear you speak again." She tossed Janet a dismissive nod and moved on to a nearby table.

Conference sessions and two more talks Eduardo had agreed to give stole away many of the hours that weekend. But Janet and Eduardo stayed up late each night, talking and clinging to each other, and managed furtive hand-in-hand strolls around the darkened campus. Janet gloried in the warm touch of his lips pressed firmly against hers at last, in the semi-privacy of a small stand of trees behind the dormitory where Janet was staying. "I feel as if I've been waiting for this forever." She clung tightly to him, nuzzling her head into his shoulder, the thick soft wool of his sweater muffling her small sniffling sounds, her arms circling his muscular chest. He kept her close, stroking her hair, chuckling softly at her tiny noises, then lifting her chin to bring his lips to hers again and again.

The conference ended. They hadn't had nearly enough of each other. They'd only just begun and it was time to part. Eduardo walked her to the bus stop on Sunday afternoon. He held her tight. "What if I didn't go back to school? What if I just stayed with you?"

"Silly girl."

He smiled, took her arm and guided her steps onto the bus. Her mad impulse vanished. She settled into her seat and managed to blow him a tearful kiss as the bus roared away.

Reluctantly, Janet returned to life as a college freshman overwhelmed by the mysteries of chemistry. It was back to sharing their lives on pathetic bits of paper. "When I landed my lips on yours it was as if I'd been starved for a year and I was given nectar," Eduardo wrote.

Touching words, romantic words, but not enough to satisfy Janet's urgent need for assurance--to know where she stood with him. In the short time they'd spent together on the campus, it had been impossible for Janet to ignore the way women were instantly attracted to him. After all, she'd been one of them. After each of his talks, they hovered round him, asking what Janet thought were silly questions, lingering even after he had answered them. He had written to her about the little troupe of girls who followed him around at Oberlin. "They mean nothing to me," he'd said. She had not been entirely persuaded.

Was she really the only one? She didn't know how to ask him. She shared her angst with Wanda, her roommate at Miami University, who came to her rescue with a bold idea. Wanda took it upon herself to write to Eduardo apologizing for the intrusion but insisting that she had to ask because she was worried about her roommate. "Janet's becoming more and more stressed and ill, and I think it has to do with you. I'm worried that she may do something bad to herself. Please, if you are only playing around with her, you must let her know. Or, if you love her, make sure she understands that. She has no one to turn to but me."

The swarm of girls that hummed round him meant nothing to him, Eduardo insisted again in his next letter to Janet. He loved only her. He wanted to see her again as soon as he could make it happen. Janet relaxed a little.

Within weeks, Winifred and Raymond learned the real reason for Janet's trip to Ohio University. One of Janet's friends had quite innocently spoken to them about how delighted Janet had been with Eduardo's speech at the conference in Athens. Her parents reacted with a shrill phone call and a lay-it-on-the-line letter insisting that she never see Eduardo again if she wanted them to continue paying for her college education.

"All bets are off. War has been declared. The shit has hit the fan." Janet was in fighting mode as she shared her parents' words with Wanda.

Libby James

Chapter 3
"We Like You, Eduardo"

Winter. Short gray days and accumulating piles of dirty snow didn't do much to bolster Janet's spirits. The Christmas holidays came and Janet went home. She did her best to join in the family festivities, but her heart wasn't in it. She kept thinking about Eduardo alone—or maybe not so alone--in Oberlin.

When she returned to school in January, she forced herself to concentrate on chemistry. Her efforts paid off and she earned a C-minus in the class. "I passed and I'm done with formulas and equations forever. What a relief," Janet said tossing her chemistry book into a trash pile. Wanda smiled. Janet changed her major to sociology.

Winifred and Raymond now knew that the time Janet had spent away from Eduardo had done nothing to take the heat out of her feelings for him. They decided they could no longer stand by and watch their daughter in the process of what they saw as ruining her life.

"We can't let this go on." Raymond mumbled from his favorite chair in the living room, loud enough that Winifred could hear. "We're going to Miami to find out what's happening. And we're going to find a way to stop this affair, once and for all."

"Maybe someone at the college will be able to help us," Winifred said.

"It doesn't seem likely but it's worth a try," Raymond replied.

Winifred dabbed at her eyes and twisted her handkerchief into a damp little knot. "It frightens me so much to think about where Janet's life is headed."

The Johnsons descended onto the Miami University campus and scoured the place in an effort to find out all they could about Janet's life there. They spoke to her dormitory advisor, a school counselor, the minister at the church she attended, the dean of women, and two of her teachers. The fact that Eduardo was many miles away at Oberlin and had never even set foot on the Miami campus didn't deter them. They knew Janet had schemed and lied to see him and that was information enough to fuel their mission. Some of the people they spoke with appeared sympathetic with their concerns, but no one offered them any solutions or offered to enlist in their cause.

Janet agonized. She knew her parents loved her and wanted what they believed to be the best for her. She would never be able to understand how they reconciled their religious beliefs with their feelings about race. She couldn't stop puzzling over why they were so adamantly opposed to her relationship with this man she loved so deeply. A man they had never met.

The day before the Johnsons planned to leave Miami, Raymond asked Janet to share a cup of coffee with him at the Student Center. They strolled together to a corner booth carrying steaming cups and a couple of glazed donuts, Janet's favorite. Raymond settled himself across from her, took a bite of his donut, washed it down with a swig of coffee, and wiped his mouth. "Hmmm, hmmm." He gulped and Janet could see that he was gearing up to speak. She couldn't help smiling, touched by the tension she sensed he was feeling and understanding how difficult it must be for him broach this subject with her.

"I feel like a father standing on the beach watching my child jump into a boat and head out to sea. No matter how I shout, my child pays no heed. She is entranced with the ride. I stand helpless, hoping she will have sense enough to turn back before the boat capsizes. Maybe a miracle will steer her to a safe haven."

Janet hadn't touched her donut. She was so moved by her father's words that she could not swallow a bite. This was by far the longest speech she'd ever heard come out of his mouth.   "Dad, I wish I knew a way to help you to understand. This love of mine is the real thing. It isn't going to change. It won't go away."

Following the Johnsons' visit, Janet did her best to comply with two things they asked of her. She met with a counselor. "You are in love with Eduardo's problems, his dynamic personality, physical ap-

16

pearance and intelligence," the counselor told her. "You are in love with freedom. You allow him to touch you because you respect him, but you are not in love. Go out and fall in love with a white boy to replace this non-love of yours."

Janet was disturbed at the counselor's words but she made herself think about what he had said. She decided that she didn't know what love was if it didn't grow from all the reasons the counselor had mentioned to her. What right did he have to tell her that she was not in love, she wondered. In response to her parents' other request, she forced herself to have a few awkward dates with white boys.

*****

Summer heat. With her first year of college behind her, Janet found herself continuing a painful battle with her parents. They threatened to wield the financial stick they had been dangling over her head for months. If she persisted in loving Eduardo, they would quit paying her college expenses. "It's the only way we know to get you to end your relationship with this man. Your mother and I don't want to keep you from going to school. You must know that. But we insist, for your own good, that you end this impossible relationship."

"I can't do that, Dad. I've told you. I love him. It's as simple as that." Janet clung to the slim hope that if her parents could only meet the sophisticated, intelligent man to whom she had given her heart, they would immediately understand and be overjoyed for her.

She had invited Wanda to live at the Johnson's house for the summer. Her parents were welcoming. Janet and Wanda spent long hours in conversation. "There are plenty of ways to get through college without your parents' money." Wanda was insistent. "You can get a job, go after a grant or scholarship, or do both. I know you can manage it if you have to." Janet listened, encouraged, and tucked Wanda's words away, hoping she'd not need to take the path her friend suggested.

Don, who had recently married Janet's sister Delores, teamed up with Wanda and together they approached Winifred and Raymond. "I think if you suggest that Janet invite Eduardo to your home, you may be pleasantly surprised at the result." Don gave them a conspirational look.

17

"What harm could it do?" Wanda added. "Janet would be so touched by your offer."

"She's right. What is the worst that could happen? After all, we've tried everything we can think of." Winifred gave her husband a hesitant look. "Do you have any better ideas?"

When she heard that her parents wanted to meet Eduardo, Janet could hardly believe it.

He had graduated from Oberlin in May. Janet was not at the ceremony but that did not dampen her pride in knowing that at long last he had achieved an important goal, one that had seemed unattainable for so long. He planned to enter Northwestern University the following fall to pursue a master's degree in sociology and anthropology.

In August, he took time off from his summer job in a cement plant in Elyria, Ohio and boarded a train to Indianapolis. Wanda, Don, and Janet met him at the station. After the initial joy of being in his presence again, Janet found herself part of the eerie silence that overcame the four of them as Don drove toward the Johnson's home. She could feel her heart thumping in her chest. The palms of her hands were cold and clammy, and there was a lump of something scratchy lodged in her throat.

Don pulled into the driveway and let everyone get out of the car before putting it into the garage. Janet watched as Eduardo took in his surroundings; the fragrant dogwood tree, the basketball hoop mounted on the garage, the bicycles leaned against the wall, the blaze of pink and purple petunias on either side of the walk leading up to the front door.

She wondered what he might be thinking. This place had to be light years away from his childhood home in a bush village. But then, she reasoned, he's been around--Johannesburg, South Africa, Lisbon, Portugal and now this, her home in midwest suburbia, USA.

Raymond and Winifred awaited their arrival, just as jittery as the arriving foursome. Janet was touched by the welcome her parents managed for Eduardo. Raymond took his outstretched hand. "Thank you for coming. It's long past time we met." Winifred offered a smile and a handshake as well. "Come on in," she said, holding the screen door

18

open for him.

"I'm honored to be here." Eduardo flashed his impossibly engaging smile. Janet wondered how anyone could resist him. How could anyone not be enchanted by this man, she thought. "Honored and a little frightened, to tell you the truth." Eduardo entered the house after carefully wiping his feet on the doormat. "I appreciate your willingness to have me."

Winifred led Eduardo through the front hall, asking about his trip, acting almost as if he were an old friend. "Put your things down and come help me in the kitchen." She swung open the door and led him inside.

"Sure." He turned to follow her. "Can I wash my hands?" She pointed to the sink, handed him a towel, then set him to work stirring the soup. "Watch that it doesn't boil over. It can happen fast." It began to bubble. When Winifred gave the word, he ladled it into bowls and began delivering them to the table. Janet stood by searching for something — anything she could do to look busy. She held the swinging door for him as he brought the bowls to the table and set them down with great care.

Then it was time to sit down. They gathered around the big dining room table, in this family reserved for only the most important occasions. Janet sat beside Eduardo. Raymond prayed using words that avoided any specific mention of their guest. Conversation picked up when Don asked Eduardo about his summer job.

"Never worked so hard in my life. I haul bags of cement around all day long. It's been a good change from studying, but it took some getting used to. I'd become soft. I needed a good dose of physical labor, but to tell you the truth, I'm looking forward to going back to school."

Raymond spoke up. "What are you planning to do when you finish school?"

"I'm committed to returning to Africa." Eduardo looked directly at Raymond. "I've been asked to serve as head of the youth center at the Swiss Mission in my country. Once I thought that would be a perfect job for me, but now I'm not so sure. My country is in such turmoil these days." He was careful not to mention the battle he was engaged

19

in with his supporters in Mozambique who had recently learned about his relationship with a white American woman. They were enraged by the news.

Instead Eduardo expressed his pleasure in being in an American home. "I so miss having family around. I grew up in a small village in the bush among brothers and sisters, uncles, aunts and cousins. We spent most of our time outdoors. Until I was ten, I ran free on the nearby hillside tending my family's sheep and goats without a care in the world."

After ice cream sundaes, Wanda, Don, and Delores disappeared into the kitchen and began to rattle dishes. Raymond leaned across the table toward Eduardo, taking the lead without giving Winifred even a glance. "We can see that you are a fine young man, Eduardo. We know Janet cares deeply for you. We understand that there is nothing we can do to change your feelings for each other. So, go ahead and love one another if you must, but listen to me when I tell you that nothing permanent can ever come of this relationship."

Winifred spoke slowly, gulping, clearing her throat, working hard to appear calm. "We can't tell either of you who to love. But Janet, as your parents, and because we love you, we must forbid you to marry Eduardo. You are young and naive. Neither of you can imagine how difficult this union would be for you, for us, and for any children you might have."

Eduardo sat back in his chair. He looked at Winifred and then at Raymond. He was not smiling. It was some time before he spoke. "I understand your worries and I respect your feelings." He continued to look from one to the other, nodding as if to acknowledge their words. He went on, in his deep, rumbly voice. "I know you want only the best for your daughter, but I must respectfully disagree with your assumption that we cannot have a good life together."

"We like you, Eduardo." A glistening drop formed in the corner of Winifred's eye. "Even after such a short time being with you, we can see that you are a good person. But you can't marry a white girl and Janet can't marry a black man. In many places it isn't legal, and everywhere it isn't right. There's no way that you and Janet can spend your lives together without bringing great pain and hardship to you both and to your families. We don't want that for either of you."

Janet said nothing, and with great difficulty managed to contain the wave of emotions threatening to destroy her composure and make her either scream or throw up. It was at that moment that she knew she would have to make the break with her family. She would be on her own to finance the rest of her education. I'll find a way to way to get through college without their help. By God, I will, she told herself. She didn't say a word out loud.

Chapter 4
Nice Girls Don't

Rough, damp earth beneath the old bleachers at Miami University's abandoned football stadium wasn't Janet's first choice of a place to lose her virginity. But she'd been so ready for so long that she wasn't going to be choosy. For more than two years they'd both been so restrained, so obedient to the teachings of the church and the mores of their time and place. She had no illusions about Eduardo's sexual experience. He was thirty-three and she knew too well how attractive he was to the opposite sex. And he'd been as good as engaged to Judite for a year in Mozambique before he left for Portugal. When he came to the states, he'd offered to look for a scholarship so that Judite could join him in the U.S. to study, but her father had refused to allow his daughter to leave home. It was the end of their relationship.

At long last it will be just the two of us. Janet daydreamed as she anticipated their time together. Eduardo had made plans to come to Miami for a long weekend during his first semester in graduate school at Northwestern. There would be no conference to worry about--no church camp--no speeches to give--no parents to consider.

At a small cafe a block off College Avenue, they sat next to each other on the same side of a drab brown, vinyl-covered booth and ordered grilled cheese sandwiches and Cokes. They ate slowly, savoring their food and the moment, not feeling a need for words. When they finished their meal, they stepped into the cool October night and strolled hand-in-hand toward the old stadium. The moon, a thin bright slice in the sky, made ample space for endless stars. "Funny, isn't it?" Eduardo mused. "The moon's the same but the stars are all different in Mozambique. So where is the Southern Cross from here?"

At the crumbling bleachers of the old stadium they paused, still

23

holding hands. Janet had never seen this place in the dark, but she knew, as everyone on campus did, that if you wanted a safe, secluded spot to be with your sweetheart, the dark cavern beneath the bleachers at the old football stadium was the best close-by option. The campus police stopped by on occasion, but it was generally known that they didn't check too closely if they checked at all, and were lenient toward smooching couples as long as things stayed quiet and under control.

Janet had fantasized about a cozy, warm dorm room or even the back seat of a car. But school rules plus an ever-present roommate made the dorm room option out of the question, and neither of them had access to a car. That left the stadium. Without a word, Eduardo took Janet in his muscular arms and gently stroked her long, brown hair. It was as if he'd read her mind. She smiled a little, gazing into the dark pools of his eyes, touching one lid and then the other with her fingertips, small and white against his dark skin. She felt like a child playing a game of peek-a-boo. Her hands moved up to his forehead and through the crispness of his short-cropped hair. How good it felt to be near him, close enough to be aroused by the scent of his fresh earthiness. It's so reminiscent, she thought. "I love the smell of you. It's the thing I miss terribly when we're apart."

He cradled her head in his big hands, radiating gentleness, and pressed his lips to hers, lingering there, shivering a little as he clung to her. He held her so close that she felt his trembling body and his hardness. He was as anxious as she. The world around them disappeared. The bleachers above, the football field, the cold uneven ground--none of it existed, none of it mattered. They didn't feel the damp or the chill in the air. They heard no sounds. They clung to each other, locked for these moments in a small tight place that was, for now, all their own. The rest of the world went away.

Afterwards, they lay side-by-side in the dark night, relaxed and drowsy, clinging to this sacred time, wishing that it would never end. They would have stayed there for hours if it hadn't been for a campus cop who came snooping around waving his flashlight below the bleachers. They lay stone still, hoping he'd not see them and would move on. But they weren't really worried. What had they done wrong?

What campus rule had they disobeyed?

After pausing for a moment, the cop took a few steps back then hurried off into the night. Janet let out a little sigh. They rose then, brushing away the leaves that clung to their clothes before setting off toward Janet's dormitory. On the porch, as Eduardo took her into his arms for a parting kiss, Janet heard a rustling noise, then caught a shadowy glimpse of someone in the dark green uniform of the campus police.

The next day Eduardo returned to Northwestern. Janet found a note in her mailbox asking her to report to the Dean of Women's office. Since her parents had stopped paying her college expenses, she'd been exhilarated by a feeling of independence. She had sealed her commitment to Eduardo with no regrets. She was weary from the events of the last months and aware of the battles that she feared still lay ahead. At the same time, she sensed new confidence and strength emerging in her.

She surprised herself at the twinge of sympathy she felt for the dean of women as she stumbled around trying to find the appropriate words to chastise Janet. She was visibly uncomfortable, tentative and fiddling with her pen as she referred to Janet's activities under the bleachers of the football stadium. "Nice girls don't go there and they don't do what you were doing." She let her eyes wander toward the ceiling. "It's not moral."

Amusement supplanted Janet's moment of sympathy. It was all she could do to keep from smiling. The dean seemed totally unaware of what was so regularly happening in the dark cave beneath the bleachers. She was fairly sure that the campus cop would not have reported her if Eduardo had been white or, for that matter, if she had been black.

She forced herself to look chagrined. "I promise that I'll never go there again," she said, lowering her eyes and trying to look full of remorse. With an exasperated sigh that Janet took to indicate the dean's disgust with her and the dean's relief that this encounter was about to be over, Janet got up to leave. The dean nodded a dismissal with no glimmer of a smile, no acknowledgement or understanding, not even a handshake or a pat on the back. Janet knew that she was caught in a world that wasn't going to cut her much slack. But, love, well, for her it was all worth it.

Chapter 5
Morning Star

❝ Hey Janet! Can you crank up another load of French fries? The volleyball game just ended and before we know it, there's going to be a hungry horde descending upon us." Joe, assistant manager of the burger bar in the student center, knew from experience how to stay ahead of things.

Janet put down her book and shouted, "Sure." She loaded a wire basket with fries and dipped them into sizzling oil. Since the beginning of the 1953-54 school year, her second at Miami University, Janet had been supporting herself with a small scholarship from the Methodist church and a food service job in the student center. She worked weekday evenings and still managed to maintain good grades.

The tension created by her parents' continuing insistence that she end her relationship with Eduardo took a toll on her. She was uncomfortable being in conflict with the wishes of her parents but unwavering in her commitment to Eduardo. And she missed him. When he suggested that she might consider transferring to Northwestern University, she scribbled off a note in return. "What a great idea. Let me see what I can do." Right away she began to plan.

When her parents learned that she was planning to transfer to Northwestern, they panicked. In an attempt to stop her, Winifred spoke to the dean of women at Miami. Given her "immoral" past, Winifred suggested to the dean that Janet should not be given the "clean slate" that would be necessary for her acceptance at Northwestern. "I'm sorry, Mrs. Johnson, but there is nothing I can do. She hasn't broken any rules." The dean dismissed her politely but firmly.

When Janet learned what her mother had done, her insides churned. *How long would this battle go on? When were her parents going to give up?* After she calmed down, Janet could only smile a little, amused at the thought that the dean was no doubt delighted to learn that Janet was planning to leave Miami University.

Not so easily discouraged, Winifred tried another tactic. She met with a Northwestern University admissions officer and tried to convince him that her daughter was not "morally fit" to attend Northwestern. "But Mrs. Johnson, I have only your word, no concrete proof of your daughter's immorality. She hasn't committed a crime." He refused to take any action that would jeopardize her acceptance.

And still her parents pressed on. Raymond went so far as to inform the U.S. Department of the Interior that Eduardo had "broken his contract" with the providers of his scholarship funds by intending to marry a white girl, and should no longer be allowed to study in the U.S. That quest went nowhere. The Johnsons' last-ditch attempt to keep their daughter away from Eduardo involved trying to persuade the Reverend Ralph Dodge, Secretary of the Board of Methodist Missions in the United States, to do what he could to prevent their daughter's marriage to Eduardo. The reverend politely declined to get involved.

Janet arrived at Northwestern University in September 1954 to begin her junior year. She brought with her a stellar academic record, but because she was a transfer student, she was not eligible to apply for a scholarship until she had successfully completed a year at the school. She was able to manage by finding a cheap room to rent and a job in the school cafeteria which provided her meals.

Living in the same town, attending the same school, and spending time together every day, Janet and Eduardo thrived at Northwestern. They studied together, rode their bikes around town hand-in-hand, and spent hours talking in Eduardo's small apartment. Eduardo gave Janet an African name, Nyeleti, which translated as morning star. They vowed one day to name a daughter Nyeleti.

Janet soaked up all that Eduardo told her about his past. In his letters he had often been hesitant to answer her questions about his childhood. She had wondered why. She'd been curious for so long: *Who were his friends? What were his parents like? Did he have siblings? What thoughts spun around in his young head? What did he do for fun? What were the influences that had molded him into this person she was drawn to so strongly?*

One day Eduardo began talking. It was then that Janet realized that he had not answered her questions for fear that she might be put off by some of the details, especially when he was not present to explain them. *What would she think if she knew that his ears had been slit as part of an initiation ceremony when he was a young boy? That he lived in the bush and until he was ten, herded his family's goats and cattle and had never seen the inside of a schoolroom? That his father had three wives?* But now that they knew each other so well and had the time to talk, he seemed willing, even anxious, to share his early life with her.

"In 1920, half a world away from here and fourteen years before you were born, Musamusse Mbenbela, the third wife of a Tsonga tribal chief, gave birth to a son and named him Chivambo, in honor of his tribal ancestor, a great chief. I was that son. My mother made me learn the names of all the long line of chiefs from whom I am descended. 'You must be brave,' Musamusse told me. 'You have been chosen by the gods to be the valiant lord that leads men into battle.' It was quite a load for a little boy to carry." He laughed, adding that his Portuguese name, Eduardo, was given to him later by an uncle.

"Descended from a great chief? Really? So that's what drives you?"

"My mother was a wise woman." Eduardo nodded his head slowly, for emphasis. "She could not read, write or speak Portuguese but she had an uncanny understanding of the strange pale people who ruled our land. "They may overpower us with their weapons and machines, but they cannot eat our food and they die easily from diseases," she explained to me. 'You must learn the witchcraft of the white men. To survive, you must know their language and their ways.'"

Janet sat back, finding it hard to relate to all that she was hearing. "I was born in a house where there was no electricity or running water and my dad taught me how to milk our cow," she said. "But by the time I was four, we'd moved to a bigger house that had all the modern conveniences and was a few short blocks from my school."

29

"I didn't go to school until I was ten because my family needed me to herd their sheep and goats. I watched over them as they roamed the hillside outside our village in the Gaza District. When I finally entered the government-run Roman Catholic School, I was older than the other first-year students. I was so anxious to learn that I made a pest of myself. I soon learned that the priests were more interested in having their students as servants than they were in teaching us reading and math. I hated that. One priest told me that I should learn to be a good servant. 'That way you'll always be able to make a living,' he told me. I didn't stay at that school for long."

"Did you just walk away from the place?" Janet frowned. She was having a hard time imagining a school where the teachers didn't care about educating their students.

"Once during the school day, a priest asked me to go out into the countryside and see how many young boys I could recruit to come to their school. 'I'll be missing my studies if I do that,' I told him. 'I'd rather stay here and go to class.'

'Nonsense. Do as you are told,' he said, sending me out the door.

"That was when I did walk away, headed for the hills where I knew young boys would be tending goats as I had done. I thought to myself: I cannot ask these boys to leave their herds and come to this school where they will learn nothing except how to serve the priests. And I can't do it either. I'm leaving this place.

"I entered the Swiss Mission Protestant School in the village of Mausse where my sisters attended and there I was exposed to real learning. I couldn't get enough of it. I was always the first to arrive at school, and I never missed a day. Musamusse died when I was twelve and from that time on I bounced from one relative to another. But nothing could keep me from going to school."

"That part about you hasn't changed." Janet looked around his apartment at the piles of books and papers waiting to be graded.

"To be continued." Eduardo gave her a peck on the cheek. "As a matter of fact, I need to get back to the books. And so do you."

"But I want to hear more. You're just getting started."

"There will be time, my sweet Nyeleti. I promise you."

Chapter 6
"This Marriage Will Not Work in Africa"

For a long time Janet had been sharing her parental battles with Eduardo in her letters and now face-to-face, but he had kept from her the furor growing among his mentors and supporters in Africa because of their relationship. There had been times when she thought Eduardo had not been as sympathetic and understanding as he could have been about her family's opposition, not realizing that while she had only her parents to contend with, he was under fire from a whole community of angry critics.

"It's partly because communication is so often garbled and slow-moving between here and there," he explained. "I wrote to my uncle, Ozias Bila to tell him about us and ask how he thought the family-
-my—siblings, cousins, aunts and uncles—would accept the news that I was in love with a Caucasian girl. Ozias lost no time spreading the word, to the family and beyond that I was about to marry a white American."

News traveled fast and it was in this way that André Clerc, Eduardo's loyal Methodist mentor of many years, learned that his star protégé was about to make what he believed to be a fatal mistake. Clerc had nurtured Eduardo from the time he was fourteen, a young boy new to the urban surroundings of the capital city, desperate to further his education. In an unheard of decision at the time, Clerc invited Eduardo to live with his family and had seen to it that funds were made available through the church for his schooling. He saw in Eduardo the qualities of a leader who he believed could play an important role in the life of the country one day.

Upon hearing about the relationship, Clerc worried first that Eduardo might decide not to return to Mozambique. If he did come with a white wife, Clerc and his fellow missionaries agreed, he would lose credibility among the people working toward independence. His marriage would likely be seen as a betrayal and would surely jeopardize his reputation and effectiveness, Clerc thought. He sent Eduardo a letter sharing these concerns. "How will your wife deal with a constant stream of your relatives emerging from the bush onto your doorstep?" he asked. "Where will you and your wife be able to go on vacation? And your children will be mulatto. How will they be educated?"

Eduardo shared Clerc's letter with Janet. "Clerc feels as if I've abandoned him. He thinks of me as a son and he does not approve of what I am doing. It is obvious that racism and hypocrisy are no strangers to my church or to the missionaries who serve it. Why is it that these people think they have a right to interfere in and even direct the course of my private life?"

He wrote back to Clerc: "I know some missionaries are prejudiced against any kind of social equality between my race and yours. This is a fact. But it does not mean that they do not love us, just that they have drawn a line that does not sanction socializing, much less falling in love with an African. I have stepped over that line. I can only hope that one day that line will disappear."

Clerc was appointed by his fellow missionaries to make the long journey to the U.S. to confront Eduardo and try to dissuade him from what they referred to as "a looming catastrophe." Eduardo and Janet went to Minnesota to meet with Clerc in the home of Darrell and Mildred Randall.

Darrell Randall had befriended Eduardo when he was a student in his sociology class at Witwatersrand University in South Africa. Darrell helped Eduardo win a scholarship so that he could continue his schooling. The two had stayed in touch and in time Darrell had returned to the United States and become Eduardo's confidante as his relationship with Janet progressed. For several months, Darrell had been encouraging Eduardo to share his intention to marry Janet with Clerc and his fellow missionaries. Eduardo had procrastinated, making the knowledge even more painful when Eduardo's cousin became the bearer of the news.

A small sprightly man with a jaunty, youthful look about him, Clerc greeted Eduardo with a spontaneous hug and another one for Janet. She had not expected such a warm greeting. It did not take long for her to understand why Eduardo felt so close to this man who seemed so kindly and unassuming.

While Janet helped Mildred prepare lunch, the three men found comfortable chairs in the den. Darrel began the conversation by trying to set Clerc at ease in his quiet way, assuring him that all was not lost. "Eduardo has his own life to live. We can encourage him and help him to get his education, but neither you nor I, nor the church itself, can tell him who to love. He's got to decide that for himself."

Darrell pointed out that shortly after Eduardo arrived in the U.S. he had written to his then girlfriend and assumed fiancé, Judite, inviting her to come to the states to study. "When her father forbade her to come, the relationship came to an end. These things happen. Mildred and I were both engaged to other people before we met. It's a normal thing for young people. They need to find their own way."

"This marriage will not work in Africa." Clerc stood firmly by his opinion.

Darrell shook his head. "What about the example Seretse Khama and Ruth Williams set in Bechuanaland? Their photos are pinned to the wall of every hut and shack in the South African protectorate. Native Africans have come to see Khama's marriage to a white British girl as an encouraging sign and a healthy response to painful racial laws."

Eduardo had been listening quietly out of respect for the two older men. Now he spoke up. "I believe Janet will be a great asset to me in my work. I'm convinced that the two of us will accomplish more than either of us could ever do alone."

"Eduardo has grown." Darrell smiled, acknowledging Eduardo's words. "He is no longer totally dependent on the church. But the church needs him. If we desert him now," he warned, "we are at risk of being condemned for our action one of these days."

Clerc's reply was interrupted by Mildred's announcement that lunch was ready. The mood lightened. Everyone enjoyed watching as the diminutive Clerc devoured all-American hamburgers and potato

33

salad as if he hadn't eaten in a week. "This American food is the best," he said, looking up from squeezing a big mound of ketchup onto his second burger.

As the conversation moved around the table, Janet could see that these were reasonable men. She allowed herself to feel a little bit encouraged. She thought there might be a chance that one day Clerc would come to accept them as a couple, even decide that the obstacles he saw in their way might be overcome. She thought it premature for her to try to explain to him her fierce commitment to Eduardo and to freedom for Mozambique. She knew she'd need to somehow prove herself first.

She wasn't sure how to go about doing this, but she was convinced that there would be a way. Her desire to be with Eduardo coupled with the determination she felt to earn independence for a downtrodden people, as naïve as it might seem to those older and supposedly wiser, welled up inside her, refusing to be denied. Along with it came excitement, the same feeling she remembered as a fourth grader tracing the Limpopo River on the classroom globe and imagining herself there, staring down a crocodile.

Chapter 7
Sharing the Past

❝When I finished primary school in Mausse, I had to leave home to continue my education." Eduardo had his feet up on a small stool and leaned back in his chair, savoring a break from his studies. Janet welcomed a break, too, pleased that he wanted to go on with his story.

"Protestant schools, like the one I went to in Mausse, were often targeted by Portuguese officials. Our teachers taught us to think for ourselves and ask questions. The Portuguese didn't like to foster independent thinking. One of my teachers encouraged me to read whatever I could get my hands on. He shared his copy of *The Negro* by W. E. B. DuBois with me. The book opened my eyes to the issues of slavery and colonialism and created the first glimmer of activism in me. That book has been a guiding force in my life.

"In time the Protestant schools became the training ground for an African intelligentsia. These were the people who grew up to assume leadership positions in the fight for independence. Graduates of the Catholic schools were more likely to align themselves with Renamo, the political party that opposed independence and fought to maintain colonial status."

"What a history your country has. And it is all so recent." Janet stretched, walked around the room and begged for more.

"I arrived at the Swiss Mission compound in Khovo outside the capital, Lourenço Marques, (now Maputo) with a head full of dreams, at age fourteen. I was assigned a job in the laundry at the mission hospital on the grounds. Living in the capital city on the Indian Ocean with its graceful Portuguese architecture and bustling harbor was an exciting new world to me. My job was to deliver clean laundry around the hospital. I soon struck up a friendship with a few of the nurses. Ruth took a particular liking to me. I don't know why she did this, but one day she spoke to André Daniel Clerc, the chief of the mission, about me. I have no idea what she said, but Clerc asked to meet me. He put his arm on my shoulder, gave me a big smile and made me feel welcome.

'So you are from Mausse. You must feel as if you are a long way from home. Good for you for coming here. It makes me happy that you want to continue your education.'

"'Thank you, Sir,'" "I managed. I'm happy to be here. I hope to study for the ministry one day.

"It was only a few weeks later when Clerc called me into his office at the end of the school day and approached me with what I thought sounded like a crazy idea. 'How would you feel about coming to live with my family? My wife and children would be happy to have you.'"

"You must have made a huge impression. Do you suppose it had to do with your good looks?" Janet teased.

"Who knows? I could not have been more surprised. It was pretty much unheard of at the time, taking a native black boy into your home, not as a servant, but to live with your family. I couldn't believe my good fortune. Clerc became my mentor, friend and supporter. Neither of us knew then how long a road I still had to travel to get myself educated."

*****

Both Janet and Eduardo blossomed at Northwestern. Their delight in living in the same town and going to school together inspired their academic work. They found studying even more pleasurable when they could do it together. They rarely saw a movie or spent time socializing with friends. Their life revolved around their work and their studies.

Eduardo had an assistantship and taught an introductory sociology course to ninety first-year students. At the beginning of her senior year, Janet received a scholarship to carry her through to graduation. They began to call each other "husband-to-be" and "wife-to-be." They grew more and more comfortable as they shared each other's daily lives. Their plan was to marry in the summer of 1956 after Janet had graduated.

Occasionally, there was a check from her parents in Janet's mail-box. "I think my parents send me money because it is the only tangible way they can find to let me know that they still love me. It makes me happy to know they love me and sad to know they will never condone my decision to be with you."

Janet gave Eduardo a worried look. "You know what. You are changing the way I think. I'm not so sure about what's true anymore."

"Are you sure it is me? Maybe you've been reading too much heavy stuff. Why don't you take a break and read a romance?"

Because of what she was reading and because of the long conversations Janet had with Eduardo, she found herself moving toward a view of religion more liberal than the ideas she had grown up with. In a letter home she shared with her father her growing appreciation for Albert Schweitzer, a philosopher who lived for the now, rather than for an anticipated hereafter.

"Schweitzer's assertion that one must live in the world as it is and find beauty and goodness despite its horror, appeals to me," she wrote. Raymond responded with a warning.

"Beware of agnosticism, Janet," he responded. "It looks to me that you may be leaning in that direction. Those thoughts can easily lead to the atheism that I know to be rampant in academic circles." He suggested that she turn to her bible and perhaps take a course at the Garrett School of Theology at Northwestern.

Janet would always appreciate her parents for the affection they had shown her, for their guidance when she was young, and for the love of reading they had instilled in her. She spoke of these things to Eduardo. "It's ironic. It is the reading I've done, and the talks I've had with you that are making me question my beliefs."

"Go on. Tell me more."

"I cannot believe that my love for a Negro is wrong, or that it is immoral to marry interracially. I can no longer believe in the same things my parents do."

Eduardo listened, smiling as she spoke. "You know, it was the experiences I had when I went to college in South Africa that led me to change the way I felt about religion and the institutional church.

I became so disillusioned that I switched from ministerial studies to sociology. But that's a story for another time."

"Well, okay. But I want to hear it."

The weather was warm enough for a bike ride through town and a picnic in the park. Janet pulled a package of cheese sandwiches from the basket on her bicycle and Eduardo produced a bottle of freshly squeezed lemonade. "Now, tell me about your life in South Africa."

"It took me forever to get there. I was 28 and quite impatient by the time I started college at Witwatersrand University in Johannesburg. We called it Wits. The Swiss Mission people were sponsoring me and refused to send me before they thought I was ready. I had studied English, catechism, dryland crop rotation, been a team leader for youth groups and learned how to preach in Mozambique before they let me go.

"I arrived in 1948, the same year that the apartheid laws, intended to oppress the black population, went into effect. It didn't take long before I began to see aspects of the Christian church that made me question entering the ministry. I saw a religion that took pride in its sanctity but was clearly corrupt and had split into dozens of denominations with small, insignificant differences, each prejudiced against the other.

"D.F. Malan, the first apartheid prime minister of South Africa and a minister in the Dutch Reform Church, puzzled me. I was in the middle of this spiritual dilemma. I remember thinking: *Malan goes to the parliament every day to discuss the affairs of the nation. He turns to the same Lord Jesus Christ that I do to ask for guidance. How can he condone and enforce these laws?*

"Then, for no reason that I could ever figure out, I was beaten by a white Johannesburg policeman while walking down the street with a friend one afternoon. I hadn't done anything but walk down the street minding my own business. The blows were hard enough to burst my eardrum. In the end it was all too much for me. I decided I could not study to be a Christian minister and I switched my major to sociology."

"Thank you for sharing. I need to know these things about you," Janet said. It was late afternoon now and she made a move to pack up their picnic things. They headed home for an evening of study.

A few days later, Janet was still thinking about Eduardo's struggles, how far he had come, and his determination to serve his country. *Why couldn't her parents appreciate him? Why could they not look beyond the color of his skin to his fine mind and his commitment to making the world a better place?*

She remembered the stories her mother had told about her youth in Big Sandy, Tennessee and she shared them with Eduardo. Winifred was born into a comfortable middle class lifestyle and spent her childhood in a spacious two-story frame house two blocks west of the main street of town. Everyone knew everyone else in Big Sandy. The white people lived on the west side of town where the houses and the children were tidy and well kept.

Winifred's father owned a successful furniture business. She and her brother grew up knowing their parents had 'expectations' for them that included studying hard, adherence to a strict moral code and church every Sunday.

Every morning the black women, who lived on the east side of town, walked across Main Street to cook and clean in the homes of the white people. Winifred didn't play with black children. She didn't go to school, church, or the movies with them, and there was no playground or swimming pool that would allow them to mingle.

"Aha. Now I'm beginning to understand." Eduardo gave Janet a look that she would not soon forget. "We are all products of the culture we grow up in. Change is very hard."

"The day Winifred's father died suddenly when she was seventeen and her brother twelve, the family's lifestyle came to a screeching halt." Janet went on with her story. Her mother sold the furniture store and moved to Chicago with her two children, thinking that there would be more opportunities for her children in the city. A senior in high school at the time, Winifred was not happy about leaving her friends. In Chicago, she soon fell in love with a boy she met in her Methodist youth group.

"By that time, my grandmother had become disillusioned with life in the big city and was getting ready to return to Tennessee. My parents had to marry in a hurry before Winifred's mother and brother left town. She told me she wore a bright red, knee-length satin dress, the fanciest piece of clothing she owned at the time. There was no time or money for a real wedding dress or a traditional ceremony. And afterwards, there she was, alone in the city with her new husband.

"Oh, but I'm getting off track. I was trying to explain how I have come to understand my mother's strong feelings about the separation of races."

"I get it. I'd be surprised if your mother felt any other way. Go on, I want to hear about where you grew up."

Janet explained that the newlyweds moved into Raymond's parents' house, then later into a remote little home outside the city with no electricity or running water. Winifred put up with those primitive conditions but always spoke proudly of the fact that she drew the line at milking the family cow. They were still living there when I came along. I thought milking the cow was fun."

"Hard for me to imagine. I can't picture you milking a cow."

"Oh, but I did. Until the day my dad finished a degree in engineering and found a job that allowed us to move into a bigger house with all the conveniences. I moved from a one-room school to a much bigger one and into a suburban neighborhood where there were kids to play with and a big wide driveway. That's where I learned to roller skate."

"Hmm. I've never even come close to a roller skate. Not sure I'd know one if I saw one."

Janet and Eduardo were coming to understand the circumstances that had influenced each of them as they were growing up. It was important for them to share the times the places and the relationships that, along with their DNA, had created the two people they had become.

*****

Eduardo's relationship with Janet continued to be a hot topic among his supporters in Mozambique. Those at the Swiss Mission who had been emotionally and financially supporting him for more than a decade were enraged at the thought of his commitment to a young, white American who they were sure, was in the throes of a teenage infatuation with an exotic older man. They expected Eduardo to come home and fulfill his obligations to his church and his country, but not with a white wife at his side. They feared that he would never have the respect of the people should he come home with a white woman at his side. They were saddened and angry that Clerc had not been able to change Eduardo's mind and convince him to give up the white woman he planned to marry.

This influential group of ministers exerted enough pressure on Eduardo that he seriously considered not returning to Mozambique. "There are plenty of places in Africa where I could be useful. The movement for independence is gaining momentum fast in West Africa. I could go there."

Janet listened as he tried hard to explain. He wanted to seek change for Mozambique, but he knew he could not do it without the support of his benefactors and the people in his country who had been counting on him. "How would it be if you decided not to go back to your own country? Can you so easily give up this dream of independence you've held for so long?" She was having some trouble understanding his thinking and was bothered by this alternate plan he was considering.

"If I return without the blessing and protection of the church, I'll be at risk. The Portuguese would not hesitate to harass and even imprison me if I spoke out. And I cannot be quiet when I'm faced with blatant injustice." Eduardo had talked himself into thinking that the best course might be to stay clear of Mozambique and bide his time until he could go home with some assurance that he'd be able to speak out and act freely. He knew that without protection from retaliation by Portuguese officialdom, he would likely be deported or imprisoned if he spoke out. He wasn't at all sure how or when he might be guaranteed that protection, if ever.

Eduardo felt he'd be most effective by writing about the oppressive situation that existed in Mozambique. When the world learned the truth about his country, perhaps pressure would be brought to bear on the colonial government. "It feels like I'm sentencing myself to exile, but right now I think it is a better plan than going home and risking deportation or imprisonment."

Janet sighed, put her hand on his shoulder and looked into his eyes. "I understand why you are thinking like that. Well, I sort of understand. But I hope and pray there will be a way for us to be there together to attack the colonial situation."

Chapter 8
"Something's Come Up"

B y the beginning of 1956, Janet's final semester at Northwestern, she was counting the days. The future looked bright. Eduardo's assistantship paid him enough that he was able to buy a 1950 Studebaker—and an engagement ring. The wedding was set for August. Eduardo was in the process of choosing a topic for his doctoral dissertation. They would leave for Africa as soon as he completed his degree.

"Something's come up," Eduardo said as he gave the marinara sauce bubbling on the back burner a quick stir. They were cooking up their favorite pasta meal in Eduardo's apartment on a frosty day late in January. "It's pretty exciting."

"Well, don't keep me in suspense. I can't stand it." Janet leaned across the kitchen counter, broke a handful of thin spaghetti in two and dumped it into a pot of water boiling on the stove.

"I've been offered a research position in the Belgian Congo by the Africa Committee of the Methodist Church. They want me to a conduct a field study in urban sociology. I'll get paid for my work and the findings will become the topic for my dissertation."

Janet slid the cooked pasta into a big blue bowl and placed it in the middle of the table. She listened as he went on. "There is one small hitch, though. The church doesn't want me to marry before I go. We'll need to postpone the wedding until I get back."

"And how long will that be? Janet's head was spinning, her thoughts going to the five years she'd been committed to Eduardo, to the day when she would become his wife.

'I'll be gone for a year."

"A year?" She felt ready to explode. *What about me?* she asked herself. *What about the plans we've made? What am I supposed to do while I wait for you?* He was pushing her aside to do what he wanted to do. *Will I ever be able to say "no" to this man?* she wondered. But for the moment, she did not speak.

"A year in Africa and at last a job making use of what I've learned. It's too good to be true. I'll be earning money and working on my dissertation. What could be better?"

Janet twirled her fork and took a bite of pasta. It stuck in her throat. "I'll have to think about what I'll do while you are gone," she choked out. She left the rest of her meal uneaten and disappeared into the bathroom. She couldn't remember the last time she'd cried. She locked the door, covered her face with her hands and let out a muffled howl, tears streaming down her face.

Red-eyed and blowing her nose, Janet came back to the table and sat down. Eduardo looked at his plate still piled high with spaghetti, and fiddled with his fork. "You know how much I want to marry you. You understand that, don't you? We just have to wait a little longer."

"No. I do not understand. A year is not 'just a little longer.' I love you Eduardo. I want to be married to you. I want to be with you. I want to share your work and your bed and your joys and your sorrows and I want to do all that very soon. I think I have waited long enough."

*****

In March, Eduardo lay limp, drifting in and out of consciousness in the emergency room of an Evanston hospital. Janet had been visiting her sister across town when she got the phone call. Eduardo had been in an accident. Her sister rushed her to his side where she learned that he'd been thrown out of his car onto the road, landing on his head with such impact that he had arrived at the hospital by ambulance, unconscious. Until he came to enough to let the staff know that he was a graduate student at Northwestern, he'd been denied admission to the hospital because of his color. Only when they understood his status was he admitted, suffering from a spinal injury, concussion and a deep cut on his leg. The delay could have been fatal. Some of his friends threatened to sue.

That spring Janet gave all her attention to helping Eduardo recuperate. "Don't worry," she soothed him, kissing his forehead. Concentrate on getting well as fast as you can. I'm going to make it easy for you." She fluffed pillows behind his head, sat close on the edge of the bed and began spooning chicken noodle soup into his mouth.

" Mmmm. Tastes much better served this way." He gave her a weak imitation of his magnetic smile and slid back to a prone position after a few sips of the warm soup.

Without any hesitation, Janet took over the task of cancelling his speaking engagements and meetings. She met with his professors, brought him books and papers to work on and made arrangements to cancel his preliminary doctoral exam that had been scheduled for April.

As he began a slow recovery, Janet forced herself to begin thinking about how she was going to fill her time after she had graduated and he was away. No question was raised by either of them as to whether or not he would accept the offer to work in the Congo. It had become fact.

Janet wanted to increase her knowledge about Africa. Perhaps graduate school would be an option. She wanted to be busy. Very busy. After some research and consultation with professors in her department, she learned about a graduate program in African Studies at Boston College. She applied and was quickly accepted for the following fall. Her good grades paid off. She was awarded an African Fellow Scholarship.

Winfred and Raymond came to Evanston to see her graduate but the celebration was a half-hearted affair for Janet as they refused to even see Eduardo. He was well enough to attend the ceremony and did so, being careful to steer clear of the Johnsons. "Let's keep it simple. We'll celebrate after your parents leave," he told Janet. Her parents disappeared shortly after the ceremony, kissing Janet, wishing her luck and tucking a check into her hand.

By the end of the summer, Eduardo was able to sit for his preliminary doctoral exam that had been postponed because of his accident. He was scheduled to leave for Africa in November. Janet finished a summer clerical job in the sociology department at Northwestern in

August. A few days later she was on her way to Boston.

In a strange city in a part of the country where she'd never been before, she began a new phase of her life, one that she'd been forced to choose, given the circumstances. Her first choice would have been to learn more about Africa by travelling there with Eduardo as his wife.

During her first few days in Boston, she met Elia, a Puerto Rican woman also enrolled in the African Studies program. The two seemed compatible enough that they decided to share living quarters. They found a roomy house near the campus and went looking for a couple more students to share the rent.

"I know some people in the program who are still searching for places to live. Let me check with them." Elia contacted Carrie, a missionary from the Belgian Congo, and Buff, an Ethiopian. They all moved in together and soon became a tight little foursome who often studied and shared meals with one another.

"We're amazingly compatible, don't you think, Janet said?" Elia agreed. Janet seemed a little surprised that the four of them, so randomly thrown together, got along with each other as much as they did.

"You live in a sort of international house, right?" Winifred asked in a letter to Janet. "Are you the only Caucasian in the house? Isn't that kind of strange?" Winifred could not imagine such a living arrangement and couldn't resist making a comment about it to her daughter.

Socializing with her new friends became increasingly important to Janet. Her life had taken a frightening turn. She was working hard to adjust to her new circumstances and make the best of this unexpected, unasked for opportunity to earn a graduate degree.

She and Elia had more than one late night conversation. "I've been so geared to pleasing Eduardo for so long, and the cost has been painful. I have alienated my family and lost their support because of my relationship with a black man. I'm still totally committed to him and I'm trying hard to shake the notion that I've been –at least temporarily—abandoned by the person I love."

Elia lent a sympathetic ear. "Not easy," she said. "I admire your loyalty. You must really love this fellow."

The foursome enjoyed their meals together quite often. One night

46

Janet turned up her nose at the curry she'd made that was a favorite dish of hers. "Everything I eat here has this funny metallic taste," she complained as she pushed a pile of rice around her plate, having a hard time forcing herself to insert it into her mouth. "It tastes to me like it's been cooked in metal shavings."

"Maybe it's the water," Carrie offered.

"I haven't noticed anything like that." Buff scraped his plate clean. The others chimed in, agreeing with him and praising Janet for her curry-making skills.

Janet and Eduardo resumed their letter-writing habit. Over and over, he promised her that they would marry as soon as he returned from the Congo. Being married remained overwhelmingly important to Janet. She had grown up believing that marriage solidified a relationship, made it real and lasting. She had come to the realization that verbal or written assurance of Eduardo's love for her would never be enough. She could not get beyond her need to be married to him. In her mind, only being married would once and forever more melt away her insecurity.

A few weeks into the semester, Janet noticed that her period was late. "I'm like clock work. I never miss a period and I'm never late."

Elia gave her a quizzical look, drew a hand through her hair, looked thoughtful. "Why don't you check in at the student health center, just to make sure all is well?"

"Good idea." She answered a few questions, then forced herself to relax during the examination. The check up did not take long, but Janet could feel her heart pounding in her chest.

"Congratulations. You are a healthy young woman. Your baby is due in about seven months." The doctor shook her hand and left the examining room with a broad smile saying, "Everything looks good."

"The timing could not be worse." Elia listened, a little shaken as Janet shared her news with her housemate.

"I must tell Eduardo." That was all Janet could manage to say. She placed a call. "You're going to be a father," she choked out. "I'm expecting."

"What? Expecting what?" Eduardo was confused.

"I'm going to have your child."

"Oh my God. You're going to have a baby?"

"I want to have your child more than anything else in the world Eduardo, but not now. What are we going to do?"

The line went silent. Finally Eduardo spoke. "Why don't you come back here so we can talk? I will find someone who can help us." Janet had never heard Eduardo's voice so soft, so subdued, so filled with emotion.

*****

It was dark when they drove into downtown Chicago and found the address Eduardo had been given. It led them to a poorly-lit, narrow street scattered with trash in a rundown neighborhood. They parked the car, got out, made sure it was locked and began walking toward a shabby-looking apartment building with a single slit of light coming from a ground floor window. Just before they reached the front door, Janet slumped into Eduardo's arms, dizzy and feeling faint. "I don't think I have the strength. I can't do this. I wish I could, but I can't." She burrowed her head into his shoulder.

"I'm relieved. Truly I am." He cupped her face in his hands and gently kissed her lips. "I know it's the sensible thing to do, but no, it looks like neither of us can go through with this."

They were silent on the dark drive back to Evanston. Janet put a small white hand on Eduardo's knee and with her other one wiped away a tear of her own. He focused straight-ahead, maneuvering slowly through the city streets, though traffic was light at this hour. Janet sensed that he was still nervous about driving, fearful of making a mistake after his accident. She knew that handling a vehicle did not come naturally to him, especially in the city and when he was obviously doing all he could to keep his emotions in check.

They had two days before Janet was to return to Boston. In a few frantic hours, they were able to confirm an important fact. With a feeling of relief, they learned that interracial marriage was indeed legal in Illinois. That obstacle removed, they went to the courthouse to obtain a marriage license. Janet bought a dress, remembering her mother's hurry-up wedding in fancy red satin, determined to at least wear traditional white.

Eduardo contacted Ed Hawley, a Congregational minister who had befriended him at Oberlin. "I need a favor. I need to get married. Fast."

"At your service, Eduardo. Who is the lucky bride?"

Ed had to do a bit of rearranging but he made it work. The wedding took place in the Hawley living room in the presence of a few friends from Northwestern.

None of Janet's family came. "There's not time to invite them. They wouldn't come anyway." Janet was resigned.

There was no time for a honeymoon. Eduardo went back to Evanston and Janet went back to Boston. She assumed that she would have to give up her scholarship. She approached Bill Brown, her advisor, a well known Africanist and head of the African Studies Program right away. "I've just come back from Chicago where I got married," she blurted out. "I'm pregnant. Does that mean that my scholarship is no longer valid?"

"First, congratulations. Why would you say that? This personal situation of yours has nothing to do with your status as a student or with your scholarship. I'm happy for you. Now, go home and catch up on your studies."

Janet breathed a long sigh and thanked her advisor. "I'm so relieved and so grateful to you. I really want to finish this degree."

They had agreed that Eduardo would not be changing his plan to work in Africa. She would continue with her studies in Boston. Back at her house, she shared her the news with her roommates.

"You're going to be a mama? Hooray!" Buff said. "A baby will lighten up this place!"

"Not for seven months," Janet replied. "I bet you'll be long gone before it happens."

Chapter 9
Dream Denied

Pregnant. Married. Frightened and alone. In need of a sympathetic shoulder. Janet grew closer to her housemate, Buff. They had classes together. Sometimes the gentle, soft-spoken Buff showed up in a wildly colorful African shirt—bright yellow with red and green stripes—usually over well-worn jeans and with flip flops on his feet, regardless of the temperature. His skin was a creamy tan and quite often he sported a few days' growth of stubby black beard. They began to meet in the library or student union to go over their notes and clarify class discussions for each other. Janet felt calm in his presence and uplifted by the cheerful look he always wore. "We study well together, Buff. Maybe it's because we think alike." He appreciated her help when he got stuck on an unfamiliar word, sometimes a little embarrassed, but always willing to laugh at what he did not know.

Janet talked to him about her fear of the future. He listened as she shared the depth of her feelings for Eduardo dating back to when she was seventeen. "For the last five years I've been focused on marrying this man despite painful opposition from my family that has saddened and distressed me."

"And then you had to marry quickly and under pressure."

"Yes. It happened but not in the way I'd dreamed about for so long."

"I feel so at ease with you, Buff. Thanks for listening to me go on and on. You are the friend I need right now."

"And you are the friend I need." He picked up her books and carried them home for her.

As they spent more time together, their attraction for each other became obvious to both of them. Janet tried to calm things down a bit, to keep her distance from him when she could do so without offending Buff. She didn't want to lose the comfort of his friendship. She was lonely and vulnerable and needed his attention and concern. Eduardo was her husband and father of the child she carried, but he was far away and preparing to leave the country for a year. The feelings she had for Buff surprised and confused her.

Eduardo and Janet stayed in frequent touch through their letters. Their hasty wedding had taken place only two weeks before he was to sit for his final doctoral exam. He was studying for it and was also making his way through a training course designed to prepare him for his work in the Congo. "I'm overhelmed just now," he wrote in a quick letter to Janet. I've got to complete this training course and I have to do it right now, when it is offered."

Janet read between the lines, picking up on Eduardo's high stress level. He still tired easily, the aftermath of his car accident. In her letters, she tried to reassure him. "Make sure you eat well and get plenty of sleep. Remember that you already know the material on the exam. You've been studying it for months."

Janet rejoiced with him long-distance when he called to announce that he'd passed his exam with points to spare. He finished the training course; his work in the Congo was now specifically defined; and his ticket booked for a mid-December departure. Janet could hear the excitement in his voice when he talked about his job in the Congo. "I can hardly wait to get to the Congo and begin my research. I only wish you could be at my side," he wrote.

*****

At the end of November, Eduardo received a telegram from Bishop Booth, in charge of the mission in the Congo: "Complications." it read. "Request postponement of your trip. Letter follows."

Eduardo dropped the telegram, dazed at this devastating development. He knew that his prospective employers in the Congo and his supporters in Mozambique would not welcome the news of his sudden marriage to a white woman. The Methodist Church Commission on Ministerial Training, the organization that had hired him to work in the Congo, had expressed their displeasure, as he suspected they would.

Time was getting short. On December third, Eduardo tore open a registered letter from the Congo General Conference of the Methodist Church and read it, his fingers trembling. Because he had married, the churchmen in the Congo explained, they had been put in the position of employing him against the wishes of his supporters in the church in Mozambique. "We regret that we are are not able to compromise our standing with our colleagues in the church in Mozambique. This is to notify you that your internship is hereby cancelled." Eduardo was out of a job.

He called Janet. "I can't go to the Congo," he blurted out. They say they won't allow me to come because I'm married.

She could hear the heartbreak in his voice. "Oh Eduardo, how can they do this to you?"

"They say they can't go against the wishes of their colleagues in the church in Mozambique."

"They're punishing you because of me. It's so unfair."

'This a major blow. One more crushing incident in a long line of obstacles to completing my education. I promise you that I will never accept a missionary position, nor will I ever go to Africa with the church. I'm on my way to Boston. Be with you soon."

Janet found a one-room-with-kitchen apartment in an old building owned by the university on Yarmouth Street, in a slum area of Boston. It was available at a reasonable price to married students without children. Eduardo arrived loaded down with books and papers. He soon found his way to the library at Harvard University where he was able to work on research related to his doctorate. And he began searching for a job.

After a long debate with himself, Eduardo turned down an offer from Adriano Moreira, Portugal's representative to the United Nations, to teach at the Higher Institute of Social Sciences and Colonial Powers in Lisbon with the promise of one day being in line to represent Portugal in a political capacity in the United States. He was flattered by the offer and enticed by the possibility of a high-level job in the U.S. one day, but he knew the risk involved if he took the job. It would align him too closely with the Portuguese. He'd lose credibility with those seeking independence in Mozambique. At the same time, he knew that turning down the job would count against him if he ever hoped to work with the Portuguese regime in Mozambique or decided to apply for Portuguese citizenship. He loved to teach, the pay was good and the possibility of a job in the U.S. one day made his decision painful, filled with implications for his future.

"I have a job!" Eduardo called to Janet a few weeks later, stumbling through the door into their small apartment breathless and excited, to find her at the kitchen table, deep into her studies.

"That's great news!" She jumped up and threw her arms around him, planting a congratulatory smack on his lips before he could get another word out. She knew how desperate he was to find work, not only to make a living, but to make use of his knowledge and his long years of schooling. Combined with her relief that he would not be away from her for a year was her understanding of how much the job in the Belgian Congo had meant to him and how devastated he'd been to see it slip away because of a situation in his personal life.

"I am about to be employed by the United Nations." A satisfied grin spread across his face as he hugged her tight. "From now on you may refer to me as Assistant Professional Officer in the Department of Non-Self-Governing Territories in the Territorial Research and Analysis Section of the Division of Trusteeship. I'll need an oversized business card to include all that."

He was to be based in New York and the job was scheduled to begin May 1. They agreed that Janet would stay in Boston to finish the semester and have the baby before she joined him. "I'll be home every weekend," he promised.

"I'll try to see if I can manage to go into labor on say, a Friday, for your convenience, okay?"

"That would be nice. See what you can do. A Saturday would work as well."

By the end of the school year, Janet was nearly finished with her masters in African studies. Her class work was complete and her thesis was well underway. Because they were about to be parents, they had to give up their married student housing and find a new place to live for the few months before Janet and the baby would join Eduardo in New York. When landlords learned that Janet was part of an interracial couple, apartment after apartment became suddenly unavailable. In the end, Elia helped her find space in an old house on Beacon Street that had been divided into apartments. When Eduardo left for New York, Elia moved in to stay with Janet.

When they had time for some leisurely talk after Eduardo came to Boston, he began to understand the depth of Janet's feelings of abandonment when she learned that he had committed to being away for a year. "It made me unsure of your love for me. It seemed so easy for you to accept the job in the Congo. Maybe if we could have discussed it before you made the decision, I wouldn't have been so devastated. I've never wanted to disappoint you Eduardo, so I didn't say anything at the time."

He tried to explain. "I had such a strong need to work, to make some money, to prove myself after so many years in school, that I didn't take into account what my decision would mean for you."

Janet was relieved that they were having this conversation. Her relationship with Buff had been weighing on her mind, making her feel guilty. "I was so alone when I first came to Boston, so needy. I found myself becoming close to my housemate, Buff. We saw each other every day, often shared meals, and studied together. I spilled my guts to him more than once, telling him how lonely I was, how much I missed you, how it scared me to think that you would be gone for a whole year. And he responded, describing his loneliness and longing for his home. We were a comfortable shoulder for each other."

"What has happened to us? What does this mean for our future?" Eduardo took Janet into his arms. She could feel his body trembling even though the space heater was making the small living room uncomfortably hot. "I don't understand this insecurity you have around my love for you. What can I do to convince you once and for all that I love you and I always will."

Janet's admission of her attraction to Buff, combined with the events of the past few months weighed heavily on Eduardo. She watched day by day as he sank more and more deeply into a state of depression. He began to experience episodes when he found it difficult to breathe. His heart raced out of control.

"I had to tell you about Buff. I will always be honest with you, no matter how hard it is for me to say or for you to hear. There can be no other way," Janet promised, putting her arms around his broad shoulders. "I'm worried. Let's get you some professional help.

Eduardo found a counselor who helped him to understand how the recent cascade of events in his life was impacting his mental and physical state. As he had time to reflect, the episodes of shortness of breath became less frightening and eventually less frequent. He learned to pause and quiet himself with a few moments of meditation.

He and Janet continued to share their feelings with each other and as they did, she sensed a new comfort level occurring in their relationship. Neither of them had anything to hide. On the last day of April, he patted her expanding stomach. "Promise me you'll take good care of the little one."

He gave her a hug and a lingering kiss. Janet watched as he sprinted out the door to catch the train to New York, on his way to begin his first "real job" with the United Nations.

*****

Two months later, Janet placed a call to Eduardo's workplace. She was thankful that it went through quickly. "I'm—I'm in—I'm about to have this baby! It was the first week of June, right on time.

"Gotta go." Eduardo wasn't sure who heard his words, and he didn't really care, as he blasted out the door of his office, grabbed a taxi and was at LaGuardia Airport in minutes. He was lucky that Boston-bound planes flew frequently. Within a few hours he found himself at Massachusetts Memorial Hospital, begging to be admitted to Janet's room.

"I had to persuade them to let me in. They said my color did not match up with the color of the woman in the labor room. I had to beg and plead and promise that you really were my wife." Eduardo was angry and frustrated. Janet was so drowsy by the time he showed up in the labor room that she heard only snatches of his frantic explanation. She was worried that the natural childbirth she had planned on was not going to happen.

Her labor dragged on. She eventually agreed to a spinal injection to alleviate pain a few minutes before their son made his way into the world, a bit worse for wear. "We're a family now." Eduardo beamed. We have one good-looking son." He kissed Janet's forehead and smiled into her weary eyes. "I was so sure we'd have a girl. "What do you think we should name this little guy?"

"That's an easy one. He looks so much like you, he has to have your name." Eduardo Chivambo Mondlane Jr. arrived June 7, 1957, a child of two people from vastly different worlds.

Janet had not been warned, or did not remember, the importance of remaining prone for several hours after receiving a spinal injection. As a result, she suffered fierce headaches that lasted for days after little Eddie was born.

She knew that the birthing of babies and their care and nurturing had been part of a natural cycle of life for Eduardo as he grew up in the bush. He did not understand chemically assisted births and the care of small babies "by the book" with specific reference to a popular volume by Dr. Spock that she had been studying. All this was foreign to him. Janet knew nothing of child care from personal experience and that made her nervous.

"I don't know a thing about this business of parenthood," she admitted to Eduardo. And her mother wasn't there to help.

Part of Janet's angst was related to the debilitating headaches she was experiencing. They immobilized her. She was afraid that she was not going to be able to care for her baby. She moved through their apartment barely able to function, grateful that Eddie slept a lot and was not, so far, a demanding baby. She checked his breathing every few minutes, worried that he might be dead because he slept so soundly. Her attempt to breast feed him became so painful that, without any advice or encouragement available, she quit within days. Eduardo did not understand these things.

He came home to Boston every weekend but the rest of the time Janet struggled alone trying to recover her strength and meet the demands of a newborn. Eduardo did his best to help when he was there.

"You must pull yourself together. Try as hard as you can to get a grip. Things will soon get easier", he said. "Go on to bed and get a good sleep. I'm handling the night shift."

She couldn't have been more grateful. His words helped her to get control of herself and as her strength returned and the headaches dissipated, she began to realize that she was going to be able to manage. The anger she felt at what she saw as a botched birth experience faded as she recovered. But she remained convinced that with more experienced care Eddie's birth could have been less traumatic. At the end of the summer, when she and Eddie joined Eduardo in New York, she felt like an old hand at motherhood. She looked forward to the new era in their lives that was beginning.

Chapter 10
Return to Africa

Themnew little family settled into a garden apartment in a United
Nations community in Jamaica, on Long Island. Their neighbors were from all over the world and the Mondlanes found
it comfortable and easy to develop friendships with them. They fit
well into the company of people such as Roy Wilkins and Ralph
Bunch who would one day become guiding lights in the Civil Rights
movement. They counted Muriel and Ray Belsky among their closest friends. Their children were close in age and the friendship would
continue in the years to come.

"Perhaps we should consider a second child soon." Eduardo made
a semi-casual remark during a conversation he and Janet were having about the future. "If we find ourselves somewhere in Africa where
schooling is difficult or non-existent and home schooling becomes
the only option, you will have two students close in age, better than a
single pupil."

"An interesting thought." Janet blinked and managed to maintain
her composure so that she could respond in a quiet voice, as she attempted to recover from her shock at the words that had just come out
of Eduardo's mouth. "It probably makes some sort of sense, but right
now it seems kind of--overwhelming."

*****

Eleven months after Eddie's birth, he had a sister. They named her
Chudane after Eduardo's father's first wife, known to be a strong, resil-
ient woman warrior.

With rounded cheeks, masses of brown curly hair and dark luminous eyes that dominated her petite face, Chude didn't just show up,
she roared into the world, confounding the nurses in the delivery room

with her exotic beauty as well as her energy level. They'd never seen anything quite like her. From day one she took it upon herself to make her presence known in the world.

Janet soon realized that sleep was of little interest to Chude. Instead she chose to keep the whole family awake at night, so insistently that her parents turned over their bedroom to little Eddie so that he could sleep. They moved to a couch in the living room with Chude nearby until, in a desperate search for sleep, they relegated her to the kitchen and closed the door. "As soon as someone gives her some attention, she's quiet." Eduardo had her figured out early on.

"She's not wet, she's not hungry, she just wants company," Janet agreed. Desperate, she impulsively picked up the telephone one day. "Mom, I need your help. I'm losing it. Would you consider coming here for a few days?" Janet heard herself begging. She'd sensed a softening in her mother's attitude following the birth of Eddie, and she had no one else she could ask to help her preserve her sanity.

Winifred didn't hesitate. "Of course I'll come. Just find me a place to stay." She met Eddie for the first time and was enchanted by the endearing nature of the toddler. "He's so friendly. He takes my hand. He likes me. He's irresistible." She took over the care and handling of baby Chude and still found time to take walks in the nearby park with Eddie in his stroller. She giggled along with him as she pushed him in the toddler swing, touching his tiny fingers as he swung toward her. "More, more," he shouted.

Janet began to recover her equilibrium. "Mom. I know coming here was hard for you. I'm so grateful for your help. I was at the end of my rope."

Winifred hugged her daughter, something she had not done for years. "I'm so glad I could be here." Ten days later she gave Eddie a hug and climbed into a cab headed for the airport, blowing them all a kiss as she disappeared.

*****

When the babies were one and two, Janet declared herself ready to return to her studies. She had completed her thesis and earned her masters degree in African studies just before Chude's birth, and now she wanted to work on a Ph.D. in sociology. She found daycare close by and enrolled in Columbia University, a subway ride from their home. Before she could complete the two courses she'd enrolled in, Eduardo's plans intervened.

He had secured scholarship money to complete his Ph.D at Northwestern and arranged for a leave of absence from the United Nations. Janet suspended her studies and she and the children went with him to Evanston. It only took him a few months of concentrated work to complete his dissertation and receive his doctorate in social psychology, making him the first Mozambican in history to earn a doctoral degree. In the summer of 1960, the family returned to New York and Eduardo resumed his duties with the United Nations.

"At last," Eduardo announced weeks after their return to New York, scooping up a child in each arm and squeezing them in a big bear hug as he shared the news. "Dr. Mondlane is headed back to Africa."

Janet looked up from a sink full of dishes. "Really? Tell me, tell me," she insisted, a smile lighting up her whole face.

"Finally. This is our chance to get to Mozambique," Eduardo said releasing his children and looking into Janet's eyes. "I have been asked by the UN to monitor a plebiscite in British Cameroon. In February, the citizens will be voting on the formation of a republic. My work there will take about five months, and when I'm finished, I'll go to Mozambique. You and the children can join me there."

Abandoning the dishes and drying her hands, Janet did a little jump for joy. "I'm so thrilled to finally be going to Mozambique. After all this time, I can't believe it's really going to happen." But when she took a moment to think through the scenario he'd proposed, she had an uncomfortable pang. She realized that she and the children would be left in New York to wait for months while Eduardo did his work in British Cameroon.

"Why should I stay in New York when the children and I could just as well be waiting for you in Mozambique?"

"Why should you?" Eduardo answered with a look that said I wish I'd thought of that. "Yes. We'll all leave at the same time. You and the kids can get to know Mozambique on your own. By the time I arrive,

61

you will have charmed every member of my family."

"It's settled then." Janet turned her head away and shed a silent tear. This moment had been so long in coming. She had only a couple of vague second thoughts about taking two toddlers half way around the world on her own to live in a place where she would be a stranger, feeling her way in unknown territory. But nothing could take away the fact she was on her way to the land she'd dreamed about, had been waiting to experience, for more than a decade. Nothing and no one was going to interfere with this plan, she decided.

Eduardo asked Clerc to find his family a place to stay, hopefully in the Swiss Mission compound in Khovo, on the outskirts of Lourenço Marques, Eduardo's first home outside his bush village, so many years ago.

Chapter 11
Mozambique

❝Welcome. So happy to see you!" Clerc waved when he spotted the family as they deplaned in the Lourenço Marques airport. He gave Janet a big hug. "I thought maybe you could use a little help getting through the irritating formalities."

"Oh yes. I'm so relieved to see a familiar face." Too soon Janet would learn about the Portuguese penchant for bureaucratic craziness. Nothing was simple and straightforward. Everything to do with customs and immigration would be tedious and take too long.

"It's such a pleasure to have you here. And look who you've bought along! Such beautiful children." Clerc stooped to greet Eddie and Chude who were sticking close by Janet at the moment, looking bewildered and rumpled after the impossibly long trip.

When the travel-weary little troupe finally emerged from the airport into the heat and early morning brilliance of the day, a cheer went up from a small crowd, taking Janet by surprise. A cluster of missionaries and natives had been waiting for them since before dawn. A young woman stepped out and threw her arms around Janet with abandon, then bent to welcome the children. "We are so honored to have you here." She grinned, displaying the whitest, most beautifully formed teeth Janet had ever seen, gleaming in the intense light. Marcia was one of Eduardo's many cousins. She had left home the evening before and slept fitfully on a slow-moving bus so that she could be at the airport in time to meet Eduardo's American family.

The trip to Mozambique had taken days. The first leg of their flight landed in Switzerland where they paused for a day of rest. Janet had a chance to meet with several Mozambican students who were studying there. The journey from Geneva to Lourenço Marques took 29 hours in a four-motor plane with stops in Leopoldville, capital of the Belgian Congo and Luanda, Angola. Both airports were dark and frightening places patrolled by armed men.

"I am so happy to be here at long last. It feels like a homecoming," Janet said smiling at the little group of welcomers. Within minutes, she felt a special kinship with Marcia and an appreciation for all those who had made the effort to come to the airport to meet her and the children.

"I felt from the beginning that these people knew me--that they had been waiting a long time for you, and now for your family, to come home--that we were expected, even longed for," she wrote to Eduardo, as soon as she was settled in the lodging Clerc had prepared for them.

Figuring out where to house Eduardo's family had been a challenge for Clerc. The blacks and whites who lived and worked at the Swiss Mission were housed in strictly defined separate areas on the grounds. Deciding where the Mondlane family could live without invoking the wrath of the Portuguese authorities who insisted on this separation, kept Clerc awake at night during the weeks before their arrival. He finally hit upon the idea of turning a small abandoned building that stood off by itself near the hospital, in a "neutral" part of the compound, into a place where the family could stay without offending anyone.

Janet could not help noticing how Clerc's Swiss wife, Maren, drew in her breath as she helped her unpack her trunk. Maren's eyes widened when she saw the pretty dresses, clothes of a real lady, come tumbling out. Janet could see that she was surprised, not sure what to make of what she was seeing. "What beautiful clothes you have." Maren folded the blouses neatly and hung her dresses on a rack. "These wrinkles will disappear. The humidity will help."

Maren had not expected Eduardo's wife to own a wardrobe like this one. Janet felt slightly embarrassed. It was just now dawning on Maren that Eduardo had undergone a sea change in the time he'd been away. He was no longer the naive young boy from the bush she had taken into her home so many years ago. He had married someone completely different from an African woman--someone who wore the kind of clothes she saw in Janet's trunk. Sorting through its contents became Maren's introduction to the new Eduardo, a reclassification of his status, months before he set foot on his home soil.

It wasn't until after they were settled into their quarters in the small building next to the hospital, their home for next few months, that Janet began to feel sensitive about the whiteness of her skin. Standing out against black faces wherever she went was a new sensation for her and it made her self-conscious. For the first time in her life, she was learning what it was like to be in the minority. There was no escaping what she began to think of as her "white shadow"--a reflection of her pale skin that she could not escape. She wondered if her whiteness would be a barrier keeping her apart from these people she longed to embrace as part of her family. She'd lived nearly a decade dealing with fallout from racial discrimination in her own country and now, in a turn about, racism was haunting her again as she began a determined effort to fit in to a place that she knew would one day become her home.

The white missionaries were kind and welcoming but she noted with dismay their attitudes toward the black people they lived among and ministered to. Weren't these missionaries people who had given up their homes and moved to another continent to spread the word of Christianity? They didn't seem to Janet to be treating their fellow humans as equals.

"A bit of advice, Janet. Don't sit next to the blacks in church because they are full of lice," a wife of one of the missionaries was trying to be helpful to the newcomer.

Janet looked at her unbelieving, smiled and nodded her head. As the days went by, she found herself feeling more and more black inside. Despite the white shadow that tagged along wherever she went, she felt more black than white. She pondered this strange feeling, but she could not deny it. And she didn't want to.

Would Eduardo's family accept her as one of them? She wondered. After all, she had no control over the color of her skin and she wanted desperately to find her place as a member of Eduardo's family. At least her children were black. That would help, she hoped.

"How does it feel when these black people call themselves part of your family?" one of the missionaries asked her.

"Good. Because they are," Janet responded looking straight into the woman's eyes. "And once I have learned their language, I'll be better qualified to count myself as one of them."

*****

Cooling breezes blew in from the sea each afternoon, helping to relieve the heat of the day. Even so, Janet had a hard time falling asleep at night, tossing and turning under her mosquito net. She found herself fantasizing about a humming air conditioner that did not exist. The children had no trouble sleeping after their days spent exploring new sights, listening to new sounds and discovering new playmates. Hot water did not flow automatically from a faucet, but then, not much hot water was needed in this climate. It had to be heated on a gas-burning unit like a camping stove when it was time to give the children a bath. They began to adjust.

With beginner's eyes and determined to keep an open attitude toward this place, so drastically different from anything Janet had ever known, she set out to explore the city with her children. With a child in each hand, she meandered from stall to stall at the bustling outdoor market. "It smells like dead fish." Eddie pinched his nose, reeling from the pungent odor as they approached rows of fish laid out on wooden planks with flies buzzing all around. "Let's get out of here."

And so they moved on, passing a butcher's counter where hefty chunks of raw meat lay out in the open and seemed of particular interest to the swarms of flies. "Yuk." Chude backed away. They decided on this day to fill their shopping bags with beautiful tomatoes, peppers, mangoes, bananas and pineapple.

Back at the mission compound, the kids were soon at home with the children of staff members and joined them as they played happily together in a big sandbox. One evening the Clercs took the Mondlane family to a nearby beach on the Indian Ocean. Close to the shore, fishermen gathered around driftwood cooking fires, chatting together as they waited for East Indian traders to come and buy their catch. Then they climbed into their small boats to sleep until dawn before venturing out to sea again.

66

Janet took the children to the beach often after that trip. Eddie and Chude could not get enough of splashing in the waves and watching the antics of monkeys in the trees above the shoreline. Janet came to love getting into the soothing, warm water as much as the children did. The three of them laughed as the undertow tried to tug them out to sea, sinking their feet into the sand and throwing them off balance. Janet caught the kids up in her arms holding them close, keeping them safe beside her.

The monkeys' only goal in life appeared to be snatching whatever looked appealing to them that belonged to the beach visitors and then running away with it. "Hey! That monkey stole my banana," a surprised Eddie shouted.

"Maybe he was hungrier than you are. Here's another one. Hang onto it."

Early one morning, Janet left the children behind and set out for the harbor. She knew the dreary history of the dockworkers who had struggled for years to eke out a living doing hard labor for low pay. She was curious to see them at work. South Africa and Southern Rhodesia (now Zimbabwe) depended upon the port of Lourenço Marques to ship goods abroad from their industrial and mining industries inland.

A dockworkers' strike demanding living wages a decade ago had resulted in the arrest of 500 men. The Portuguese sent fifteen of the instigators away to forced labor camps. The other protesters went back to their underpaid jobs. In the years since then, nothing had changed. Janet watched as men chatted in small groups, waiting to see if there would be work for them that day. There were never any guarantees. Many of the dockworkers had given up and made the difficult decision to leave their families behind and go to South Africa to earn a better living underground in the gold mines.

*****

Janet soon got to know Doctor Ribeiro, who practiced medicine at the mission. He saw up to one hundred patients and performed three or four operations in a typical day. He existed in a constant state of exhaustion, risking his own health because of his horrendous schedule. The people who lived close to the mission were fortunate, though. For

Mozambicans who lived in rural areas, there was only one doctor for every 9,000 people.

Educational opportunities weren't much better. Janet visited a two-room school with three teachers and three hundred students who attended one of three shifts each day. Sitting in a falling-apart plastic chair in the back of a poorly-lighted classroom with totally bare walls and a single small blackboard, Janet was touched as three girls and two boys, ages nine or ten, sang a song in her honor. Their uniforms were clean, but worn and too small, their faces animated, their voices strong and clear. When they finished, they bowed to her and went quietly to their seats.

Janet scanned the silent room with children squeezed into row after row of rough wooden benches. No one pushed or shoved. No one made a sound. No feet shuffled. She wondered if they ever acted up, just a little. As she left, she noticed another group of children gathered under the shade of big tree for a science lesson, who seemed just as well behaved. *They don't have a discipline problem here*, Janet thought. These were kids who knew they were fortunate to be in school and they weren't going to do anything to jeopardize that privilege. She was told that very few of them came from families that would be able to pay the fees that would allow their children to attend secondary school.

*****

Dismayed by the shabby condition of the student dormitories at the Swiss Mission School, Janet found a bucket and brush and set to work. The missionary staff looked a little shocked when they saw the newly-arrived white woman on her hands and knees scrubbing and cleaning. Janet didn't care. She found some paint and without asking, began to give the dorm a fresh new look. Maren noticed. In a few days she appeared with yards of fabric and began sewing new curtains for the dormitory rooms.

After they had been in the country for a few weeks, Janet and the children were invited to a Mondlane family gathering in their honor. The relatives were curious. Many had not had a chance to meet the family yet. A cousin was chosen to give a formal welcome. He warned

Janet that as Eduardo's wife, she would have certain duties to perform for the older women who were now her relatives. "You'll be washing dishes, fetching water from the well, pounding mealies and cooking porridge," he promised, being careful not to crack a smile. The relatives waited a little nervously to see how she would respond. Janet wished more than anything that she could respond to them in Portuguese. She was taken with the young man's sense of humor and his picturesque way of expressing himself. A translator, she decided, is a poor substitute for one-on-one getting-to-know you conversation, especially when it comes to humor.

In the eyes of Eduardo's sister, Vaselina, Janet could see Chude's luminous eyes. "Now I know where you got those eyes," she told her little daughter. These people are our family. They want to be friends with us. And Janet wanted, in the worst way, to be able to communicate with them, to tell them how happy she was to be among them.

Back at her desk in the small home at the Swiss Mission she shared with her children, Janet sat down after the children were in bed, to tell Eduardo about the experiences she'd had with the white missionaries and with his family. The struggle she felt burning inside her loomed large. "My skin is white. People think I am white. I know. I look white but I feel that I am part of the world that is black. Why are there two worlds? There should be only one. Perhaps you and I are here on this earth to become a bridge between the two.

"The whites here forget that I am married to an African. That an African has my heart in his hand, that an African knows the dearest secrets of my soul. That a black man is the one I sleep with, who kisses me in the morning and at night, who laughs with me, with whom I quarrel and whom I love. That it is this black man that gave me my children. I don't think I felt black before I came here, but I feel the whites pushing me away from them. I'm afraid that when you see me, when you remember what white people do to black people, then my white skin will disgust you."

Chapter 12
"Only You Can Answer"

Janet agonized over what she learned in Mozambique. For the natives, life under Portuguese rule was close to intolerable. People struggled every day simply to survive. Changing the regime, getting out from under Portuguese rule, she came to realize, was the only possible answer. Average income hovered near a dollar a day. Health care and education were woefully underfunded. Most students had no opportunity to study beyond primary school. Jobs were scarce. Conditions were ripe for revolution, enhanced by the winds of change that were blowing across all of Africa. It wasn't hard for Janet to visualize Eduardo playing a major role when the time came for change. She was anxious to join him.

"The missionaries will support an independence movement," Clerc assured her.

"But who will be the force firing up the independence movement?" Janet asked. "It seems to me it is going to take natives with more at stake to do that. As the most highly educated Mozambican, with many years' experience as a political activist, savvy in the ways of the Portuguese, Eduardo seems a logical choice to take the lead."

Clerc smiled. Janet understood that he agreed. Even more important than his education and experience, she saw Eduardo's uncanny ability to unify disparate groups of people as critical to the effort. From what she had learned of his background, going back to his early childhood, she knew he had always looked beyond the welfare of his own tribe. Something innate in his makeup made him understand the need to encompass the larger community—one that included his region, country, continent, and even the world at large.

Only a strong and skillful leader would have a fighting chance to unite the various fragmented freedom movements into a force capable of working together to overthrow the Portuguese. There were those in the infant freedom movements that saw Eduardo's choice of a white wife as a detriment, Janet knew. They questioned whether he could command the credibility and gain the support needed to bring a grass-roots revolutionary movement into being.

But those who doubted Eduardo's capacity to be effective underestimated his charisma and his ability to influence others. Janet had faith in him. She knew the depth and strength of his vision and his powers of persuasion. The doubters had no way to know about the extent of her commitment to the cause of freedom or her growing conviction that despite her pale skin, this middle-class American white woman was deep inside a black revolutionary. With every day that she spent in Mozambique, she became more passionate about joining the movement to achieve independence.

*****

After Janet read Eduardo's latest letter, she did her best to comprehend his words, then put them out of her mind until morning so that she could get to sleep. But she could not. Sleep would not come. The more she thought about his words, the more distraught she became. Her mind tumbled into a steep, furious spin. There was nothing to do but crawl out from under her mosquito net and go searching for pen and paper.

Columbia University had tracked Eduardo down in British Cameroon and offered him a prestigious permanent position on their faculty. "I have accepted." His words scratched across the white page like black pinpricks into Janet's soul. "We'll be leaving Mozambique a month earlier than we'd planned so that I can start my new job on time."

She shivered in the warm night. Her hands shook as she twiddled the pen in her fingers, wondering how to start this letter. She knew how much this man loved the academic life. How he was in his element when he was teaching. How good he felt among young people. How thrilled and flattered he must have been by this offer. How much he felt at home in New York. This job was a dream come true for him.

She knew all these things, but still she did not understand the decision he had made. And she was angry that he had made it without consulting her.

Once she got started, the words flowed onto the page faster than she could scribble them. "I don't know what to think about you. You are a brilliant intellectual caught in a situation in relation to your country that disturbs you mightily. I know you would rather teach than do anything else in this world, but can you really choose teaching when a choice must be made between shaking this colonial system and that teaching? Only you can answer that."

Eduardo replied the same day he received Janet's letter. The envelope contained only a copy of the letter he had just mailed off to Columbia University. In it, he apologized for his need to reverse himself and decline their offer. He did not try to explain why.

He had no illusions about the enormity of this decision. He knew that it would shape the course of his and his family's life for years to come—probably forever. There would be no turning back.

Chapter 13
Home at Last

"Dad's here! Dad's here!" Eddie and Chude came running across the compound grounds. "Mom, dad's here!" Hauling a tattered brown suitcase, Eduardo was doing his best to keep up with his kids. At the last minute, he'd been able to catch an earlier flight. No one had been at the airport to see him take the first step onto his native ground after a decade-long absence.

Eduardo held Janet close, as he juggled to include Eddie and Chude in his embrace. Janet's head was spinning, wondering what it must feel like to him, to be back home after so long. He had become a different man. He'd earned three degrees, married, fathered two children and now worked for an international organization. His countrymen and supporters had been observing him from afar, not always agreeing with the steps he took, but now counting on him to guide their country through whatever it was going to take to achieve self-rule and a brighter future.

The lifestyle that Janet and the children had been living at the Swiss Mission disappeared when Eduardo arrived. Gone were the leisurely hours when Janet could ponder her impressions of the place and the people. These days there was no time to meander through the local markets or play with the children on the beach.

Wherever Janet and the children went with Eduardo, people crowded around, anxious to touch him, talk to him, tell him their stories. They came to the compound hoping to get a glimpse of him; better yet, have a word with him. Janet watched as he embraced the people, listened to them and came away sobered by the fury he heard in their voices, at the oppression that ruled their lives. She saw that they looked upon him as a savior.

And wherever Eduardo went, there was the PIDE, the Portuguese Secret Police. They stood on the street corners and hid in the trees on the Swiss Mission grounds. For the first time since she'd been in Mozambique, Janet was careful to keep the children close, to look behind and ahead, around corners and in the bushes, constantly on the alert for something that didn't look right.

"They will watch us, but they don't dare harm us," Eduardo assured Janet. "As long as I am in the country as a representative of the United Nations, we are safe."

Soon after he arrived, Eduardo went to Ritkala, the town where he had been a youth leader many years ago, and discreetly called a meeting of the black pastors there. He wanted to gauge their level of commitment to the fledgling underground liberation movement.

"We're with you 100 percent." A spokesman for the group sounded totally committed. "We're ready to do what it takes to become free. Anything you say."

But when Eduardo asked if these pastors would be willing to move to Tanzania, across the northern border of Mozambique, to establish a fighting force, they became quiet. One of them spoke up. "Must we leave our homes to do this? I'm not sure we can see our way clear to taking such a drastic step. It would mean leaving our jobs and being separated from our families."

"And it would involve some danger. Perhaps it is too much to ask." Eduardo nodded his head but kept his gaze on the group. "But that is what will be required." These men were hungry for independence, but still they balked at upsetting their lives. The sacrifice that would be needed was frightening and too great. It was more than they could see their way clear to become involved with at the moment.

A church service in Eduardo's honor in the village of Chamankulo drew a crowd of Catholics, Protestants and Muslims who came to praise him in poetry and song. Janet could not understand what Eduardo said to them in Portuguese, but she saw that their adoration of him was palpable, vibrant. And the thought crossed her mind that now, revered among his own people, in the land where he grew up, she wouldn't be surprised if he might be having second thoughts about her, wondering just how and why he had come to marry this pale white woman and create a family with her. She forced herself to put aside such troubling thoughts.   For the moment, she made herself relax and appreciate the welcome these people were showering on her husband.

Eduardo planned a month-long trip around the country with Janet and the children. Reverend Ralph Dodge, the Methodist bishop in the diocese that included Mozambique and part of South Africa, knew Eduardo and was aware of his mission. In a gesture of support, he offered the family the use of his Chevrolet station wagon to make the trip. The day before they were to set off, Clerc came to Eduardo. "I've just received a phone call from a man who would not give his name. He says the Chevrolet has been rigged with a bomb."

"Let's go and check it out." Eduardo didn't look too worried. He found the driver and together the three men checked the car inside and out, crawling underneath it, looking under the hood and seats and inspecting every possible space that a bomb could have been stashed. They found nothing. Eduardo got behind the wheel and took the car for a spin, to make sure.

Clerc checked with the Portuguese governor general who insisted that no one he knew would ever do such a thing. Then the governor personally guaranteed the family's safety for the trip. Janet relaxed a little, but still she wondered how this governor was able to offer this kind of guarantee for their safety.

The driver remained doubtful. Eduardo assured him. "Look, I wouldn't think of taking my two small children on this trip if I thought it might endanger their lives." Reluctantly, the driver agreed to go. Janet, who had been standing by listening, calmly collected the children and their things and climbed into the back seat with them.

Any worries about bombs were soon forgotten when they stopped at a little roadside stand to buy bananas. The word was out. In moments, people recognized them and crowded around calling out words that translated to "welcome king," cheering and clapping. Eduardo moved among them smiling, clasping their hands, patting them on the back. "It is so good to be home." He kept telling them how happy it

77

made him to be back in Mozambique. "I feel like a new man. I've been away too long."

They stopped several more times to shake hands and acknowledge well-wishers before they arrived at the Swiss Mission in Chicumbane, across the Limpopo River from Joao Belo, capital of Gaza, Eduardo's home district.

Natala, an old woman who Eduardo immediately recognized, sat soaking up the sun in front of her little concrete home. Perched in a worse-for-wear plastic chair that seemed on its way to disappearing into the ground on which it rested, Natala looked up to see her former pupil. She blinked, hardly believing what she saw. Eduardo made his way close and grasped her hand.

"This lady took me from the bush where I did not see anything and started me on the journey to where I am now." He folded Natala's hands into his, kneeling to look lovingly into her eyes, as she squinted into the sun.

"Now we are praying that you and your wife will come and free our country." Natala, still clinging to his hands, pleaded. It was soon obvious that she was unable to stand but she made no mention of it. Janet knelt down beside her.

"He was bright and he loved to learn. I only had six years of school myself when I began teaching under that old ndsondso tree." She pointed a bumpy finger at a huge gnarled tree with great spreading branches. "Eduardo was one of the oldest children in my class. He never missed a day of school, never."

Natala wasn't through talking. Her English was surprisingly clear and easy for Janet to understand. She eased herself onto the ground beside Natala. "After teaching for eighteen years, the mission honored me with the gift of a trip to Switzerland. When I came home, I moved to the village of Antioka, just down the road from here, and began working with girls and young women. I developed youth groups where they learned all sorts of practical things—cooking and childcare, sewing and gardening.

"At Antioka, one of the teachers was jealous of my success and put a spell on me. Twice I fought off a herd of cattle that he sent to destroy my field. The third time I threw rocks at the ox he sent, but I fell and could not move. After six months in the hospital, I came home, but I could never move my legs again."

Janet didn't know what to make of this tale. *Was it a dream? Was it Natala's way of explaining her paralysis?* Natala had long ago accepted Christianity, but in her explanation of what had happened to her, Janet realized that she had retained the mysticism of her indigenous religion and clung to it as part of her belief system.

"Thank you for teaching Eduardo. You did your job well. He has not forgotten what you did for him."

Eddie and Chude were as excited as Janet was to cross the Limpopo River. Right here before them was the reality that had once been no more than a thin wavering line on the classroom globe Janet had traced with a small finger as a fourth-grader, dreaming about what it would be like to see this great, grey, green greasy river. They made the crossing on a small barge powered by men standing on a creaky raft pulling mightily on a rope tied to the far side. The river flowed swiftly around the barge, close to flood stage. Eddie lay on his stomach near the edge of the barge, allowing the green water to run through his fingers. "Oooh. It feels so cool. I wish I could jump in."

Every few years the river overflowed onto the surrounding land, drowning cattle and ruining houses and crops, Janet learned from one of the bargemen. Fortunately, this year the dams in South Africa had been closed in time to prevent flooding in Mozambique. The fertile Limpopo Valley was forever at the mercy of the South Africans. In times of drought, they closed the floodgates and kept the water for themselves. When it rained too much, they released the water and the fields in Mozambique flooded.

Eduardo pointed out to Janet the lush valley where, in 1954, the Portuguese had established Colonato de Limpopo and began to send unemployed workers from Portugal to settle there and cultivate rice fields on land that belonged to the natives. Since Eduardo had been away, the population of the area had doubled. Fourteen hundred Portuguese families were now living in the Limpopo River Valley.

When they arrived in Jao Belo on the other side of the river, Eduardo reported his presence to Oscar Ruas, the Portuguese governor of the district. Ruas lost no time inviting Eduardo into his government plane, anxious to fly him over the area and point out the agricultural progress of the last decade. "Look at our flourishing farms. Everybody has jobs here. We are prosperous these days." Ruas smiled with pride. Eduardo looked closely at the farmland below, no longer being worked by its rightful owners, the Mozambican natives. He took careful note but was careful not to react and to refrain from sharing his anger with the governor.

That evening the Portuguese dignitaries, Swiss Mission people, Eduardo's cousin, Joao Mapangalane, now chief of Manjacaze, and a nationalist leader, his wife, and Matheus Muthemba and his niece, Josina, sat down with the Mondlanes to a table set with fine linen, sparkling silverware and crystal goblets. Soon this group of people would have neither the time nor opportunity to gather and break bread together. Matheus and Josina would move to Tanzania to play critical roles in the fight for freedom. The others would take one side of the political fence or the other to endure the long struggle that lay ahead. But for this moment the tone was light, the food and liquor were delicious and plentiful. No one talked of political matters.   Eduardo offered a toast. "To the welfare and prosperity of my homeland and its people." Everyone cheered and raised their glasses. Janet was touched by the event. Whatever the future held, this would remain a treasured memory. She could see that the evening meant a great deal to Eduardo as well.

"At long last I'm killing my homesickness. I should not have stayed away so long."

Janet smiled at him. "It's true. There's no place like home. I'm so glad you are here at last."

Eduardo's parents had been dead for a long time, but there was no shortage of aunts, uncles, siblings and cousins to welcome him and embrace him, to erase his homesickness.

"I'd forgotten how much this place means to me." Eduardo allowed himself a moment of pure nostalgia.

Cousin Joao, his wife Assineta, and their children moved out of their house so that the Mondlane family could have a safe and comfortable place to stay. The concrete block structure had two bedrooms, a sitting room and an all-around veranda. Cashew and mango trees surrounded the place and offered welcome shade. Pigeons, ducks, turkeys, hens and their chicks wandered about, scratching for whatever they could find to eat.

The Mondlane children were getting to know the members of their large African family. Janet noticed that kids don't suffer the way adults do when they don't have a common language in which to communicate. Eddie and Chude were delighted to be taken by the hand or even carried away in small arms to play among the chickens, try out an old tire swing, and scold the pesky monkeys for their food-stealing ways. Chude squealed as a tiny monkey grabbed her cookie and made off with it. "My cookie!" she shouted. Within seconds, one of the children had placed another cookie in her pudgy little hand.

The family went together to pay their respects at the graves of Eduardo's parents outside of Mausse, only steps from his boyhood home. A crowd of women greeted them at the graveyard, singing and dancing a dance of happiness. "Thank you for coming," Eduardo said to them. "Thank you for your support. I have brought my children here so that they can see where I was born and grew up and understand something about their grandparents."

One of the women stepped forward and presented Eduardo with a spray of fragrant frangipani, a flower that the people believe gives one the strength to face tough challenges. The other women came close and surrounded him. He could see that they wanted to talk. "We want to know about the movement for independence. Are you home for good? When do we begin the fight for our freedom?"

"Be patient. We must bide our time. Change will come. I must return to the United States for a while, but I will return as soon as I can. Meanwhile, it is best that you do not try to contact me. Even writing a letter is not safe. The secret police are everywhere and something bad could happen."

Eduardo's cousin Virgilio hosted a joyous family gathering highlighted by the slaughtering of an ox. "A whole ox? Really, will it all get eaten?" Janet could not visualize such an amount of meat. She smiled when she thought back to her family picnics where the biggest chunk of meat was more often than not a hot dog.

Eduardo's uncle, Ozias Bila, conducted a children's choir in a rousing concert. Even the youngest, at three and four years old, joined in shaking tambourines made from bottle caps, pounding tiny drums and strumming hand-held thumb pianos. The air was alive with music and the sound of small voices raised in song. Eddie and Chude chased around with the children, dancing to the music and jabbering away in English to anyone who would listen to them. Every so often, Janet heard one of them attempt a word in Portuguese.

When they drove from Eduardo's childhood home back to Mausse where he had attended the Swiss Mission School with his sisters, Janet realized what a long trek he had to and from school each day. And when she saw village boys herding goats on a hillside outside the village, she remembered that Eduardo had once spent his days in these same hills making sure the family goats and sheep were safe.

Trouble with the Portuguese was nothing new to the people in this district who had been harassed on and off for most of their lives. They had been forced to grow crops, raise animals and sell them to the Portuguese at prices so low that they could barely eke out a living. In a park overlooking a lake near Manjacaze, the knarled trunk of a huge old nsdondso tree displayed a plaque commemorating the place where Ngungunyana, the great enemy of the Portuguese, had planned an attack in 1895. His forces were defeated in battle by the Portuguese and Ngungunyana was exiled to the island of Sao Tome, never to return to his home.

Not far from the plaque, a small stone had been inscribed to commemorate the Portuguese soldiers who had lost their lives in battle with the mighty Ngungunyana. The local people saw Eduardo as a figure much like their legendary hero, confident that the leader who could set them free from the tyranny of the white man was now among them.

Janet's heart filled with pride as she heard him tell those he spoke to of his support for them. He promised over and over that change would come. She was aware that the secret police lurked here and there, watching their every move, taking note of everyone Eduardo spoke with. But they took no overt action. Their continuous presence made Janet nervous. She lay awake at night worrying about her family's safety and wondering if it had been a wise thing to bring the children on this trip.

After they left Joao Belo, Eduardo learned that the PIDE had called a public meeting and threatened anyone who they learned had decided to follow Eduardo would be executed in public. To let the people know that they meant business, the PIDE arrested Jao Belo, Eduardo's cousin who had allowed the family to stay in his house. He was held for several weeks, the PIDE's way of demonstrating to the people what could happen to them if they decided to support to Eduardo.

The Mondlanes visited the Methodist Mission at Cambine where Eduardo had studied English and taught dryland agriculture long ago. Janet was overwhelmed by the stark beauty of the remote, rural area enhanced as the sun brightened the sky following a gray day of rain and clouds. A vivid rainbow greeted their arrival. Bishop Dodge headquartered in Cambine when he came to Mozambique, and it was the car he kept there that he had loaned to the Mondlane family for their trip.

Eduardo was delighted to reunite with Samuel Sengo, with whom he had studied English at Cambine nearly twenty years before. "Samuel, you look just the same. After all these years."   Now a teacher at the school, Samuel strolled toward him down a small ruttcd path with a bounce in his step and his arms flung wide to embrace his old friend.

"I can't believe how good it is to see you. Where have you been all this time?" Samuel was more than a little curious.

After his old friend's crushing hug, Eduardo caught his breath. "I've been all over the place trying to get educated. Finally got the job done."

"Remember how hard we worked trying to master the fine points of English? What a crazy language! I'll never get it just right." Samuel grinned. "Meet my wife."

The men introduced their wives to each other and while the women smiled and tried out a phrase or two in each other's languages, the men

83

launched into memories that brought the laughter of old friends enjoying a moment to reminisce. Neither of them spoke about the future.

Janet agreed with Eduardo that it was important for them to cross the border into Southern Rhodesia and visit Salisbury, the capital, in hopes of meeting with Bishop Dodge. The trip added several hours to their journey but they were able to spend time with the bishop and also meet with a small group of activists planning a strategy to achieve independence from England. "These men will be valuable contacts for us one day." Eduardo understood the delicate art of aligning himself with people who might be in a position to help him when the time was right.

In Salisbury, which would be called Harare after independence, when Rhodesia became Zimbabwe, they attended a church service where Uria Simango, a Mozambican Congregational minister, preached the sermon. One day he would play a role in their future.

On the hot, dusty return trip to Lourenço Marques, Janet dozed in the back seat, an arm around each child. A loud scraping noise jolted her awake. "What's *that*?" She jerked upright and checked to make sure the children were all right. When she looked up ahead, she saw with horror that the front bumper of their station wagon had become hooked to the underbelly of a huge truck and they were being dragged helplessly down the rutted dirt road. After about 500 meters--it seemed more like miles to Janet—the bumper flew off and the vehicles parted. The truck moved down the road, probably unaware of what had happened. The event put Janet over the edge. She collapsed, slumping down in her seat close to losing consciousness. The children began to cry. Lack of sleep, miles of travel on primitive roads, security threats and the strangeness of it all had caught up with her. She spent the rest of the trip back to town in a daze.

Back in Lourenço Marques, Eduardo insisted that she check in at the Central hospital. The diagnosis was a respiratory infection and exhaustion. After a night in the hospital, she spent her last week in Mozambique recuperating in bed in the luxury of the elegant Portuguese Polana Hotel. "I feel so weak and useless," she confided to Eduardo.

"Don't be silly. This is a great chance for me to enjoy the kids." He took them swimming in the hotel's outdoor pool, shared fancy meals with them, waited on royally in the hotel dining room. They made several trips--to the bustling art market and to the beach to swim and to play in the sand and watch the monkeys frolicking in the forest near the shore.

Alone in her hotel room, Janet had time to engage in some serious self-diagnosis.

...I am suffering from an emotional reluctance to realize that the thing I would like to do most would be to pick up a machine gun and kill every Portuguese in sight...They are a slimy group of hypocrites with a big smile on their faces and a knife in each hand. My mind is not used to hating people, and I refused to believe I could have such negative feelings. (I'm basically a pacifist.) But once I discovered my urge to chop a few heads off, my own head attached itself back onto a healthy body and here I am.

The family had seen enough, heard enough, done enough. Eduardo's long-held hope that there might be a non-violent solution for ridding the country of its colonial status had died. Face-to-face with that reality, he knew another path had to be taken.

Chapter 14
"What Are We Doing to These Children?"

The family spent two carefree weeks in Switzerland on their way home. Janet felt her strength and health returning. She loved watching Eduardo interacting with Eddie and Chude, as if he had nothing more important on his mind than chasing them around the little park near their hotel. Chude screamed with joy as her dad caught her up and tossed her into the air. "Help, help." She screeched with fear—and with joy. Eddie watched quietly until his turn came and he flew even higher but managed to keep his cool. Janet sensed these times would be rare as she and Eduardo embarked on the course they had set for themselves. She resolved to store these memories in a place where she could hold them close forever.

Eduardo had counted on being posted in New York when he returned to his job at the United Nations. "I'm hoping to stay with the UN for as long as I can. I want to be able to lay the groundwork for the liberation front and do my job at the same time, for a while at least."

Janet nodded. "It will be pretty frantic, but if anyone can do it, you can." When Eduardo learned a few days later that he'd been reassigned to work with the United Nations Economic Commission in Addis Ababa, he reported the news to Janet with misgivings. "There's no way I can orchestrate this liberation movement from Ethiopia. I'm going to have to quit my job." With sadness and regret, he turned in his resignation. He began to put out some feelers in search of a part-time teaching position that would give him the flexibility he needed to support his family and at the same time take the first steps toward orchestrating a revolution.

Janet smiled, knowing how much he loved to teach. They were both happy when he was invited to take a temporary assistant professorship in sociology at Syracuse University in upstate New York. "Perfect. I'll have time to teach—something I love doing---and tend to my other business at the same time. Couldn't be better."

By this time Janet knew her husband's mode of operation all too well. He was going to need someone with her organizational skills to hold everything together. She figured her duties might range from keeping track of his appointments, juggling his speaking engagements, making his travel plans and seeing to it that he didn't pack for a fund-raising trip to Scandinavia without a single pair of socks. She was anxious to lighten his workload in any way she could.

She figured she'd be good at these tasks. And she was. She liked being intimately involved with the work he was doing but early on made a decision. Looking up from his increasingly full calendar, she announced, "I'm not going to any more political meetings with you, Eduardo. Instead I'm going to become your sounding board. I'll listen to whatever you tell me and hope I can offer you some helpful per-spective."

When Eduardo needed to sort out his thoughts, he depended on sharing them with her. Together they discussed pros and cons and sought reasonable conclusions. She began writing up the notes he took and his analyses of situations, and when it was necessary, she made sure that his messages reached the people who needed to see them. Her skills and willingness to devote her time and energy to arranging his life made it possible for him to sandwich his political work between his teaching duties and survive. Neither of them knew how long this set-up would last. These were heady days. One country after another in Africa was securing freedom from colonial rule and struggling to establish viable governments during their first shaky years as indepen-dent countries.

Eduardo returned from a demonstration in New York staged by Mozambican students studying in the U.S. It was discouraging for him to see that the American government was working to convince the American public of the dangers posed by an emerging revolution in Mozambique. The U.S. had an important airbase in the Azores, islands owned by the Portuguese. The Americans worried that if they displeased the Portuguese by supporting Mozambique's independence movement, they would lose the right to operate the base.

"I admit, I'm surprised, Eduardo told Janet. "I know the Portuguese and Americans are allies and loyal to each other as members of the North American Treaty Organization, but don't the Americans realize we are fighting for our lives, for our independence, that we must find a way to govern ourselves? I know the U.S. wants to keep their airbase in the Azores secure in order to defend Israel, should that ever become necessary, but don't they see the intolerable situation we face in Mozambique?" Janet listened and learned. She was getting a fast-track education in the ins and outs of international politics.

*****

Nine months after the relaxing few days they spent in Switzerland on their way home from Mozambique, in January 1962, Janet gave birth to a baby girl. They called her Nyeleti, (morning star) Eduardo's affectionate name for Janet during the days they spent together as students at Northwestern University. Nyeleti joined the Mondlane family with very little fanfare. There was no time for drama. Janet had a brief labor and delivered her third child without complications. "I feel wonderful," she told Eduardo a few hours after giving birth. "Nyeleti is a little angel."

"I fear for her, and for you," Eduardo said, holding his day old daughter against his chest. "I only wish we had the time to welcome this little one into the world without the burden of all this work."

"No matter. She's going to bc independent before she learns to walk. She doesn't have a choice." Janet was coming to terms with the way their life was unfolding.

In days, Janet was back at her desk arranging Eduardo's schedule and making appointments for him to meet potential supporters. Little Nyeleti joined Eddie and Chude as children in a family where they were much loved. But there were times when their parents addressed their political work with such urgency that the children had to come in second. If they sometimes felt abandoned, it was because that was true. When Janet left the three of them with friends in New York in June when Nyeleti was less than six months old, she felt a mix of emotions.

89

She was off to Tanzania with Eduardo to lay the groundwork for a revolution, *not a task most young mothers are called to embark upon*, she reflected. "What are we thinking, Eduardo? What are we doing to these children?"

"We made a choice. We can't turn back now. All we can do is hope that all goes well and that we are soon finished with this deadly business." His half-smile had a touch of sadness.

"I know you're right. I just had a mother's moment. Our kids will grow up strong and they will always know how much we love them."

*****

When they arrived in Dar es Salaam, Tanzania, staging ground for the liberation front, they took the first small steps in what would become a momentous undertaking. Janet testified before a UN Committee visiting in Tanzania to assess the refugee problem. There were 50,000 Mozambicans living in the country, some of them stranded there when the Portuguese closed the border, and many who had left their homes in Mozambique in fear of persecution and imprisonment by the Portuguese.

Janet got to know many of the young refugees, living in a camp where one meal a day was the norm. They were idealistic and determined to complete their education. Three teenage boys walked seven miles to meet with her and to inquire about going to school. "We heard that there might be some scholarships available. We need to go to school."

"All I can promise you is that I will do everything in my power to help you. I'm new at this job, but let me tell you, I admire your wish for more education and I'm going to do something about it."

Within days she set about finding teachers in the area. When she couldn't find enough of them, she pitched in herself to teach basic math and reading in a small, makeshift building. She couldn't get over the desire these young people had to learn. They'd been forced to leave their homes, live in a refugee camp and survive on minimal food. And still what they cared about most was going to school.

A couple of Harvard students in Tanzania for a year agreed to teach some classes. English was not the native tongue for any of these students who were of various ages and educational levels. Janet could see that her first task would be to improve their English language skills to the point where they could benefit from a full curriculum. They struggled with the language but showed amazing persistence.

She was able to raise enough money from friends and acquaintances--private supporters in the U.S.--to provide each student with a shirt, a pair of pants, and a pair of shoes, and to increase their food allowance. *They can't learn if their stomachs are rumbling for lack of food. It's an educational expense*, she reasoned.

She set to work looking for funding and eventually was able to obtain scholarships from the U.S. government for twelve of the young refugees to study abroad. Wherever she saw a need, she proceeded to see what she could do to meet it. At the time, she had no idea that she was planting the seeds for what would become the Mozambique Institute. It would serve the educational and medical needs of the refugees and the freedom fighters for more than ten years, until the struggle for independence was over.

In Dar es Salaam, the Mondlanes found themselves drawn into a tangle of political intrigue. Competing parties and organizations that grew out of tribal loyalties among the Mozambicans struggled with each other for power. It was often impossible to distinguish politicians whose first concern was the people they served from those who were out to line their own pockets.

From the time when Eduardo had resisted the demands of his Catholic school teachers that he learn to be a good servant rather than study reading and math, to his days organizing young activists in Johannesburg and Lourenço Marques, Eduardo had been preparing himself for this day and this work. Janet became intensely aware of the worldview he held that allowed him to set aside petty feuds and tribal loyalty and look beyond them to work for the good of his whole country.

Until she was thrown into helping to establish a liberation front, Janet had not given a thought to how a revolution actually came into being. She grew up in a country whose revolution and independence from its colonizers was so long ago that it was nothing more to her and her schoolmates than words in a history book and a fireworks-filled

91

celebration on the Fourth of July. She had never felt oppressed by a political system, never felt a need to fight for the freedom to speak, gather, work or vote. She had never been denied educational opportunities because of her ethnicity. But she caught on fast. Out of necessity, she learned to plan, recruit, fundraise and do a bit of political schmoozing, surprising herself at how happily she took to it all.

Eduardo found himself mired in the conflicts that arose as various entities vied for leadership of the newly developing liberation effort. His goal was to mold them into a single cohesive movement; a task that at times appeared to be impossible. One after another the leaders of these groups rose up to object, to threaten to abandon unification talks if their desires were not met.

Julius Nyerere, president of newly independent Tanzania, supported Eduardo as he sought to seek unity among the groups. With Nyerere's help, Eduardo eventually brought the vying factions together long enough to form the Liberation Front of Mozambique (Frelimo). They set a date in September when the members of Frelimo would convene to work out a detailed structure for the new political party.

So far, Frelimo was only a piece of paper. Real unity and a valid organization were a long way off. Guiding principles were yet to be defined. They were just beginning to seek the funds they would need. Yet Janet could see that for the moment it was enough. She and Eduardo returned to Syracuse in July of 1962 with an unwavering faith in the importance of what they were doing that seemed to make all things possible.

Eduardo took a two-year leave of absence from Syracuse University. He was now free of his teaching duties but unsure of how he was going to support his family. Janet took the lead in soliciting funds, working from her home in Syracuse and traveling to meet potential in the U.S. and abroad when necessary. She contacted any individual or organization she thought might have an interest in supporting their work. She met with Senator Robert Kennedy and the former governor of Southern Rhodesia, Garfield Todd, the American Quakers, the Rockefeller and Ford Foundations and the Phelps-Stokes Fund that had provided Eduardo with a scholarship to complete his education.

Janet was further introduced to the tangled threads that affect political alignments when she learned that the U.S., even under president John F. Kennedy, who appeared to be in favor of independence for African countries, continued to be hesitant to support Frelimo. "Eduardo, I don't understand. How can my country, the number one advocate of democracy in the world, not give us their support?"

"The U.S. is afraid. They're not willing to risk the loss of their airbase in the Azores. Their commitment to Israel outweighs their willingness to help us. That's just how it is." Eduardo was ready to look elsewhere. Janet felt encouraged when she was able to secure funding to develop a school from The Ford Foundation. But after a year they withdrew their support, caving in to the American government who continued to fear retribution from the Portuguese.

*****

When Eduardo returned to Dar es Salaam for the September meeting of the fledgling Frelimo Party, he was delighted to find that the factions had managed to keep their internal squabbles at bay. The first congress of Frelimo went so well that Eduardo wrote to Janet: "I felt like I could cry with joy...the crowd was simply crazy. Oh how I wish you were here to share with me both the work and the pleasures of seeing our people united."

In March 1963, Eduardo moved to Dar es Salaam to stay. He was greeted by a raucous hero's welcome, only to learn within minutes that the old internal strife had raised its ugly head again. Ever supportive, Julius Nyerere came to Eduardo's rescue, helping him to negotiate a truce between the vying factions of Frelimo. They were able to calm things down and maintain a united political party focused on fighting for independence.

*****

After a long and contentious day, Eduardo returned to his hotel in Dar, encouraged but exhausted. In the hotel lobby he encountered a group of Peace Corps volunteers staying at the hotel on their way to remote postings in Tanzania. In the group he spotted he spotted a familiar face. "Charlie, imagine seeing you here! The young man paused for a moment, then recognized his sociology professor from Syracuse

University.

"Dr. Mondlane, what are you doing here? A hug and a smile later, Charlie introduced him to his fellow volunteers.

"How about we all have a beer?" Eduardo pointed the way to the hotel bar. Soon he was chatting with the young people, asking where they were headed and what their assignments might be in Tanzania. When it was his turn to explain what he was doing there, the reality of his new status became starkly real. He was no longer an academician, theorist and intellectual. For better or worse, he was about to instigate a revolution and he told them so. He was about to make his mark in the history books.

All kinds of challenges, responsibilities and tangible, close-up danger lay ahead. But at this moment the stress and weariness of his task and of the difficult day he had spent melted away.

"You kids have revived me." He raised his beer in a salute to them. "You know, we are very much alike. Our tasks may be different but all of us are out to change the order of things, to do what we can to enhance the lives of others, whether it be through community development in a remote Tanzanian village or for the people on the sublime coastline, in the mountains, plains, cities and towns across my country that have been suffering for way too long."

"We're starting a great adventure," Charlie said. "Right now we are full of unanswered questions, but we too want to make a difference in any way we can." The students went on their way, like Eduardo, uncertain, a little frightened, but anxious to confront whatever the future might hold.

*****

Back in Syracuse with the children, Janet missed Eduardo's presence and the exhilaration of being in the middle of the action in his fast-paced world. She would not be away from it for long.

Chapter 15
"Itty Bitty Specs in Space & Time"

66 Will Dad be there to meet us when we get to Tanzania?" Eddie asked. He'd been miserable since Eduardo had been gone, weeping at the smallest disappointments and not sleeping through the night. More than once Janet had taken him into her bed to sleep with his hand in hers.

"He will be there. We'll all be together again." Janet pulled him close, thinking she must never overlook the sensitivity of her oldest child. By spring. the family's bags were packed and visas, passports and immunizations were in order. Janet had rented out their house and sold the family car.

Her sister, Delores, came to Syracuse to spend some time with Janet and lend a helping hand with last-minute details. "I can't believe you are really moving to Tanzania." They had taken a few moments to sit down with a glass of wine on the porch. The spring air still held a touch of coolness but it felt good to be outdoors. Delores took a sip. "How long do you think you'll be there?"

"However long it takes to get this revolution over with. It could be six months or six years—maybe more. You've been such a help, Delores. I'd have been in a mess without you. What can I ever do to thank you?"

"For starters you can tell me what in the world I'm going to do about my daughter, your niece. At thirteen Cindy is a mess, miserable at home and at school. She doesn't like herself. She won't study. She hangs around with friends that aren't good for her and she only goes to school when she feels like it. Don and I can't seem to agree on how to help her. In fact, we fight about it."

Janet twirled her wine glass in her fingers, rocked back and forth in the porch swing, then turned abruptly to Delores looking as if she'd had a revelation. "This may sound a little off-the-wall, but hear me out. Cindy could spend a year in Tanzania with us."

"In a war zone?

"Now, Delores, Dar es Salaam is a civilized city. Any fighting, when it happens, will be across the border in Mozambique—nowhere near us. And there's a good international school in Dar that Cindy could go to." Delores reached over to the coffee table, filled her glass, sat back and thought about Janet's generous and unexpected offer. Why don't I give Don a call and let him have some time to think about it?"

He didn't think for long. His response took Delores by surprise. "Getting Cindy away from her environment could be a good thing for her. There's no doubt it would be good for us as well. Why don't we see what she has to say about the idea?"

The evening wore on. The children had dinner and were packed off to bed a little earlier than usual. The sisters broke out a second bottle of wine and settled into either end of the couch in the living room. Janet seemed eager to continue their talk. Hesitantly at first, she began to share fears she had kept to herself for a long time. "I can't get beyond this insecure feeling. Why do you suppose it is that in the back of my mind, there is always this concern I have that Eduardo will one day be unfaithful to me? I'm a reasonable person and these thoughts are not reasonable. But I can't deny that they haunt me. How am I going to put them to rest?"

Delores didn't speak for quite some time. Then she looked directly into Janet's eyes and asked: "Are you sure your thoughts are not reasonable? Is it your intuition, or something more than that, telling you something that you just don't want to know?"

Janet frowned. "No. I don't think so. That's what haunts and confuses me. But I know this much. Eduardo is tired of hearing me beg for assurance of his love. I even do it when I write to him."

Janet went on and Delores listened.

"Eduardo keeps asking why I worry. He thinks that, in some strange way, my fears are the way I choose to express my love for him. Does that sound a little crazy? He can't figure out why he is so confident of my love for him when I seem so uncertain about how much he cares for me." She reached into a plastic box marked "letters" and pulled out one that sat on top of the pile. "Listen to this from his letter. 'Perhaps my tendency to flirt with girls explains why you dream that I am unfaithful. Surely you don't believe I am serious when I interact with these women. My hope is that your disturbing dreams are based only on the desire you have for me, especially now that I am away.'"

"You can't let your thoughts torment you, Janet. Take it from your big sister. You've got so much else to think about right now. See if you can at least tuck those fears into the back of your mind. Give it a little time. You will soon be together again and it will be easier."

Janet gulped the last of her wine and set her glass down. "I'll try. I'll really try."

Time was short. Cindy made up her mind in a couple of days. "Anything looks better than where I am and what I'm doing right now. "What do I have to lose?" she told her mom.

Delores was torn at the thought of her daughter leaving home at such a young age. "I wouldn't let you go with anyone but Janet. Wherever you are, I know you'll be safe with her."

When Cindy arrived in Syracuse, Janet sat her down. "Ready for an adventure? I know you haven't asked, but anyway, here's a bit of travel advice from your aunt. I've noticed that wherever I go, I take myself along. You are going to find that people all over the earth are quite the same. The excitement you feel, the fascination you have with new places, grows from inside you, from your attitude. Whatever happens, open yourself up to the world around you. I'm so glad you're going with us. The kids will love having you and I will too."

Eduardo and Janet had been exchanging their usual stream of letters during this time as he engaged in the tricky business of structuring Frelimo, raising funds, calming internal squabbles and forging critical relationships with foreign governments. Janet was amazed when she learned that nine African countries had agreed to donate one percent of their annual budgets to the Mozambican liberation effort. "This kind of support makes our efforts seem real, even doable," he wrote.

In the same letter, in the midst of all he was doing, he found a moment for philosophical reflection. "The challenge of the day is tremendous for you and me. We are a couple of 'itty-bitty' specks in space and time in relation to all humanity. Still, I am often awed by the consequences of our actions as they relate to the people of Mozambique, to Portugal and to the human race. We are insignificant when cast against the rest of the universe but the consequences of the words I utter these days make me wary of what I say. I see a vital line that ties us to the rest of time and space."

Chapter 16
No Easy Answers

Janet and the children, Cindy, and Betty King, a woman Janet had hired at the last minute as her secretary, to help with the accumulating paperwork, broke up their trip, as had become the Mondlanes' habit, with a few days of rest in Switzerland. While she was there, Janet met with Jean-Paul Widmer, consul general for Mozambique in Switzerland. He and Eduardo had been friends for a long time. Janet knew him from their previous trips to Switzerland. Eduardo had asked Jean-Paul and he had agreed, to take charge of the family's financial affairs during this intense time. Janet expressed her appreciation to him. "It is so good of you to help us. Dealing with money has never been Eduardo's strong suit, nor mine. Your willingness to help us is a great relief."

"My pleasure. It makes me feel good to know that I'm contributing to the liberation effort in some small way." Neither Janet nor Jean-Paul chose to put into words what they both understood--the danger that lay ahead as the war effort got underway. There was no point. Talk would not change anything.

*****

Janet lost no time diving into her work bringing the Mozambique Institute to life. Even before the children were settled in school, before the family's furniture had arrived, she and Betty were setting up an office and making plans.

Determined to have a safe haven for his family, Eduardo had found a comfortable home with an ocean view in Oyster Bay, an affluent suburb of Dar es Salaam bordered on the east by the Indian Ocean and its wide sandy beach. The Mondlane children were in their element, and if given the chance, would have spent all their days swimming in

99

the waves and frolicking in the sand.

Their new home was spacious and airy with a wide porch surrounding three sides shaded by a fragrant jacaranda tree covered with purple bell-shaped flowers. In the late afternoon, the sea breezes arrived bringing the sweet smell of salt water and helping to lessen the heat of the day. A grove of jasmine trees graced a back corner of the garden. Chude called it the smell good place.

When she learned that the nearby international school had no space for Cindy, Janet asked around. Cindy's best option seemed to be a small boarding school a couple of hours away in northern Tanzania.

"What do you think?" Janet was hesitant to make the suggestion. She had wanted Cindy to live with them in Dar. "The school has students from all over the world. It could be an exciting experience for you."

"It's a long way away." Cindy needed some time to think about being off on her own in a country she'd never heard of until a few weeks ago. But there didn't seem to be another good option. She agreed to go. "You have so much to do. I wouldn't see you much anyway," she told Janet.

*****

The Mondlane children had challenges adjusting to a new home, a new neighborhood and school, and a culture that seemed light years away from their home in Syracuse. Janet worried about how she was going to meet the needs of her children and at the same time nurture the development of the Mozambique Institute. It seemed the task had chosen her. She accepted gladly, though, happy to know the role she was to play in supporting the war effort. *Can I find the energy and the hours in the day to do it all? The last thing I want is for my children to suffer because I can't tend to their needs.* These were her thoughts as she helped Chude slip on her backpack and waved goodbye to Eddie, doing his best to smile as he climbed into the car headed for his first day of school.

There was no time for Janet to sit around thinking. Figuring out how to confront the education and health needs of the Mozambican refugees in Tanzania became all-consuming. Of the 50,000 people who had crossed the border from Mozambique and the many more who were pouring in, she knew that most of the young men, and some of the women too, would be assuming combat roles in the revolution. But until it was underway, they were clamoring to work on their education.

Janet focused on continuing the work she had begun establishing classes when she was there the year before. In addition to their native tribal language, the refugees spoke Portuguese but needed lots of help with reading, writing and speaking English. Mozambique's pathetic education system under Portuguese rule had left them without a solid foundation in the basics, something they needed if they were to move ahead with their studies.

She quickly established a board of directors for the Mozambique Institute, inviting Tanzania's minister of education and director of development and planning to be part of it. She pursued a relationship with the Afro-American Institute, UNESCO and Makerere University in Dar es Salaam and saw to it that the Institute was a registered entity in Tanzania. Betty King, who proved to be a skilled administrator, lightened Janet's workload and became her friend and confidante in these busy days.

During the entire decade of the Institute's existence, its close relationship with Frelimo kept it under an uncomfortable cloud of scrutiny. Wherever Janet sought funding for the Institute, the issue of its relationship with Frelimo arose. Donors balked at supporting a group engaged in armed conflict. "We are a humanitarian organization," Janet insisted. "We are building schools and medical clinics, not waging war." She emphasized over and over that all Institute funds were spent on humanitarian efforts and were kept totally separate from Frelimo.

As the wife of the president of Frelimo, the revolutionary front behind the war effort, Janet was in a difficult position. She could insist that The Mozambique Institute would never be an active player in the armed conflict. But because it existed to serve the needs of the freedom fighters, it was suspect. It became a tricky business to avoid even the appearance of being associated with the war effort.

101

Hoping for help in solving this dilemma, Janet wrote to Jean-Paul Widmer, for some guidance. "There's no getting around the fact that I am the wife of the president of Frelimo and that our organization provides schooling and medical care for revolutionaries. There's no denying that we are closely connected with Frelimo. How can I convince potential donors that the Institute is a humanitarian organization totally separate from Frelimo?" she asked. "The fact that Frelimo is insisting that all students at the Institute spend a year in military service makes us even more suspect."

Jean-Paul pondered Janet's words. "There are no easy answers," he replied. "I suggest you go about your business and be scrupulous about keeping your finances separate. Frelimo has to do the same." Making things even more difficult for Janet to solicit funds was a rumor floating around that both she and Eduardo were CIA agents. The accusation was common at the time, often aimed at Americans working abroad and concocted to destroy a person's credibility.

"Totally ridiculous," was all Janet had to say. When she received an anonymous letter suggesting that her life would be at risk if she did not admit to working for the CIA, she responded with what was to become typical of her attitude when confronted with such threats. "I can't be intimidated by a threatening letter. I refuse to live in fear. The best way to handle this kind of thing is to quietly continue our work." Betty had to agree with her.

Within weeks after Janet's arrival in Dar, fifty Mozambican students were enrolled in an enlarged education center. Vacant buildings close to the center were being remodeled into a dormitory to house 104 boys and 16 girls. Additional classrooms were on the drawing board and Janet had arranged for informal English language tutoring sessions for anyone willing to attend. By September a small library had opened on the Institute grounds. Then Janet turned her energies toward developing a health clinic. Because of the lack of funds, that project got off to a slow start.

In the first year of its existence, the Mozambique Institute had been largely supported by a grant from the Ford Foundation. Janet counted on the Foundation's continuing support but the following year, despite

Janet's pleading, the Foundation withdrew funding. "We have a small but thriving primary and secondary school, a library and a health clinic," she explained. "Please make it possible for us to continue our work. We have plans to establish a small hospital in southern Tanzania where we will be able to train nurses."

She understood but was frustrated by the fact that her plea was denied because of a political situation involving the American government. The Ford Foundation had acquiesced to the demands of the Kennedy administration fearful of offending the Portuguese. Janet was bitterly disappointed.

Chapter 17
A Poem

On a mellow night at home, while sipping after-dinner coffees, Eduardo and Janet were alone in their garden, gazing at the full moon over the ocean, enjoying the tranquility of the moment. The children were in bed and neither of their parents had an obligation on this balmy evening. Eduardo breathed a sigh. "Ah, what a pleasant interlude." He moved close, taking Janet's hand in his.

"And how rare." A slow grin spread across Janet's face as her eyes met his.

"Here we are, doing what must be done. You're thriving, Janet, making huge progress. I couldn't do any of this without you."

"You must know how the work invigorates me. I'm fulfilling a dream, and best of all, I'm doing it with you, and to make a difference for your people." Janet flipped her hair over her shoulder, moved closer and put her head on his shoulder.

Eduardo's thoughts were on the next few months, even as he savored this special time with Janet. "It's a shame that this work we do together forces us to be apart so much. My travel schedule is going to be crazy for the next few months." He ran his fingers gently through her hair.

She winced, sensing a familiar burning sensation in her stomach when she heard his words. She dreaded nights alone. "That's no surprise," she whispered. "Tell me about your plans."

"I'll be home until mid-October when I go to the U.S. for a month, then Germany, Geneva and China before I come home for Christmas. Next year is a big one. I leave the end of February and won't be home until early June."

Ouch, Janet's stomach responded with a pang. Aloud she said:

"That's a very long stretch. Fundraising?"

"Yes, and raising awareness of what we're doing here. I'll be in Addis Ababa, Lagos, Accra, Liberia, Tunisia and Moscow. If I don't have some substantial funds raised by then, well, what good am I?"

Janet coped well with a frantic work schedule during the day when Eduardo was away, but the nights were always hard. Too often her dreams made real the nagging fear that Eduardo had not been, or someday would not be, faithful to her. Far too easily, her imagination ran wild when he was an ocean and a continent away. In the darkest hour of the night, she was often haunted by a technicolor vision of Eduardo unlocking a hotel room door with a sleek young blonde draped over his shoulder murmuring sweet nothings in his ear.

When he was away, the mail brought a continuous stream of letters from him, but still she dreamed. He even sent her a couple of love poems, one he titled *Idle Thoughts to a Nymph*. She clung to the line that described her as "a beautiful maiden, loveliest among the lovely, young and supple as a woodland nymph."

One day Eduardo cabled Janet from Geneva, asking her to find a certain document he needed. In the course of rummaging through his haphazard pile of papers, she came across another draft of the *Nymph* poem. This one was dedicated "to Heidi" in Eduardo's handwriting. That name was familiar to Janet. Eduardo had told her about the tall, attractive, 18-year-old German girl he'd met in Geneva. He had even asked Janet to find some work at the Institute for Heidi, and a place for her to live. She had agreed to do so.

Finding the poem brought Janet face-to-face with her fears. No longer just the product of her wild imagination, there before her was evidence of Eduardo's infidelity in black and white. She wasn't willing to confide her discovery to anyone, not even Betty. Instead she sat down immediately to express her pain to Eduardo in a letter.

He answered. "You accuse me wrongly. I admit to being attracted to Heidi. It was stupid of me to send her a poem I wrote for you. But nothing ever happened between us. I love only you. Let me remind you that I continued to love and respect you in spite of what happened between you and Buff in Boston. Regardless of what you think did or

106

did not happen, you owe me that same respect."

After a few agonizing days living with her racing thoughts, Janet acknowledged to herself that she had no resentment toward this young woman. She faulted only Eduardo for giving in to temptation and for being insensitive enough to recycle his pathetic poetry. True to her word, she made arrangements for Heidi to stay with friends in Dar. She told herself that insisting that the girl not come to Tanzania would be petty, selfish and unproductive. *I will go on with my life, bury myself in my work and try as hard as I can to ignore this pain*, she decided.

It wasn't until several weeks later, when Janet was on her way to the U.S. to attend her brother Chuck's wedding, that she was able to write to Eduardo without anger. She knew that he was soon due to return to Dar and she wanted him to know that she would be back to continue her work.

What must he be thinking now? She wanted to believe that he had realized the enormity of his blunder. *Perhaps he was wondering how he could have been so stupid. What had he done? What if he was about to lose the love of his life over a silly poem? Or had he decided that she was ridiculous not to know how much he loved her?*

*****

Janet was delighted to be with her family. The tension that had persisted between her and her parents for so long had dissolved with the passage of time. She felt comfortable sharing her life in Tanzania with them, except for her current marital distress. And she could laugh with them.

Sally, mother of her brother Chuck's bride, was alone in the Johnson house when Janet's sister Delores arrived for the wedding, wearing jeans, hair mussed and wind-blown from a long car trip.

"Oh, you must be Janet." Sally was sure that this disheveled woman had to be the "odd sister who'd married a black revolutionary and lived in Africa."

Janet, who had stopped overnight in New York to go to the hairdresser and don an elegant outfit, caused quite a stir when she entered the upscale hotel, site of the rehearsal dinner.

"But you can't be Janet!" The sight of this chic young woman took

Sally by surprise. Everyone laughed.

"You can't always tell a book by its cover." Janet flashed Sally a smile.

While she was in the states, Janet learned that her first European fundraising effort, made while on her way to the U.S., had been successful. The World Council of Churches had pledged enough money to the Institute that they would be able to begin construction of a clinic near the fighting front in southern Tanzania. Her work was going well. She convinced herself that she had no time to dwell on the precarious state of her marriage, forcing herself to stay calm. She would enjoy this family time and then go back to Tanzania and concentrate her energy on her work and her children.

By the time she returned to Dar es Salaam, Eduardo had left for Prague and Berlin via Geneva. Janet didn't allow herself to dwell on why he had chosen that route.

Chapter 18
Armed Struggle

Under cover of the night, a small band of guerilla fighters crossed the border from Tanzania into Mozambique. They moved through the bush, creeping quietly through rough terrain, prepared to use guerilla tactics learned during months of training in Algeria. The Frelimo fighters took the sleepy guards at Portuguese administration headquarters in the Chai zone of Cabo Delgado by surprise. Eight of them died. The guerillas disappeared into the night and were back at their home base before dawn. This tiny operation on September 24, 1964 had no noticeable military effect but it was symbolically important. It gave notice that the armed fight to end colonial rule in Mozambique had begun.

*****

Janet attacked her work at an ever-more-furious pace. She didn't take a break until she took the children to Kenya for the Christmas holiday to visit Ray and Muriel Belsky and their children, friends from their days in Jamaica, Long Island during Eduardo's time with the United Nations. Their children were the same ages and had become friends. It was quiet and peaceful at the Belsky home in Nairobi. Janet basked in the luxury of being with old friends and having time to relax.

But after a few days, her mind got the best of her and she fell apart. One morning she awoke dazed and shocked to realize that she was in trouble. She simply could not move enough to get out of bed. Chude knocked on her door, then crept into her room to find her mother tearful and shaking. She ran downstairs, calling for Muriel.

"I have no idea what's the matter with me," Janet mumbled as she pulled the pillow over her head and slid farther under the covers. Chude was in tears by now. Muriel gathered the three children and took them to the kitchen for breakfast while Ray carried Janet to the car in her nightclothes and delivered her to the emergency room at Aga Khan Hospital in Nairobi.

Within a day, Janet had recovered enough that she could move. No physical reason could be found for the temporary paralysis and heart palpitations she had been experiencing. She was released from the hospital and told to take it easy. "I'm so embarrassed. I have no idea what came over me. I feel terrible for causing you all this trouble."

Muriel welcomed her back to the house with a hug. "I'm just glad you were here with us, in a safe place where there is a good hospital. I think your stress level just built to a breaking point."

Janet sent a letter off to Eduardo. "Right now I'm feeling inadequate to help in your life's work. I need to talk to you, to sort out my feelings. But please, be totally honest with me. Say what you truly think and feel. Can we make it together? I think I love you too much. My worst nightmare is to be the cause of your dissatisfaction, your unhappiness."

After a few days, Janet's heartbeat had slowed to nearly normal and she and the children went home. Within hours after they arrived, she found a letter from Heidi addressed to Eduardo, postmarked from her home in Germany. Janet hesitated only a moment before she ripped it open. It discussed the details of a meeting they were planning in London, on Frelimo business. It was easy for Janet to conjure up a vision of Eduardo romancing his eighteen-year-old girlfriend in London, a place where they would both be anonymous. Then he would send her off to do her duty for the cause in Dar es Salaam.

"I've decided to leave you." Janet made her announcement in a two-sentence letter to Eduardo. He responded fast, begging her to come to Geneva so that they could talk.

"I can see no reason to come to Geneva," she replied. "Finish your work there. Time is no longer important to me. Every minute is the same empty span."

Weeks later when he came home, they waited until evening when the children were in bed before they confronted each other. "We've been spending too much time apart," Eduardo began. "It hasn't been good for our relationship."

"Perhaps you do love me, Eduardo. Most of the time, you act as though you do. My problem is not knowing how many others you love as well. Until now, I have not been able to live with that."

"It's like beating a dead horse, Janet. How many times do I have to tell you that I love only you? You are the only one I love. The only one. I admit it. I like young girls. I flirt with them, even send them poems, but I keep my love for only you." Eduardo was trying hard to keep his voice down.

"I have to believe you." Janet looked into his eyes as if she might find some revelation there. "I don't have a choice. I love you too much to do anything else." Her mind had accepted his words as the truth but there was a place in her gut that would never know the real truth with certainty. It was at that moment that she decided it didn't really matter, that she could learn to live with the ambiguity. Suddenly, like a small cloud swooping down from above, a sense of peace descended, folded itself around her and she knew she had found a way to move on.

"My love for you is like an iron bar, Eduardo. It is strong and it is forever. I beg you not to pound on it too hard just because you know it will not break. There is no escape for me. My feelings for you are just there, as they have been since I was seventeen. As I told you so long ago, this love I have for you just is. It always has been, always will be, like the love of a child, a lover, a grandmother—the beginning and the end."

Janet wasn't surprised when Chude told her she'd been awake while her parents were talking. Seven at the time, she lay awake listening to their voices, not catching many of their words. She was old enough to understand that something big and frightening was going on downstairs but she wasn't sure what. Her dad's voice would soften for a while but then it would become loud and sound angry enough to give her a queasy feeling in her stomach. She heard him say something about love, about how he had always loved her mom, that he had never loved anyone else, not ever. "There are lots of women I like, and they like me," she heard him say, "but I love only you." Then the voices became too quiet to hear at all, and Chude drifted off to sleep.

Janet and Eduardo came to an agreement. From now on, whenever they could make it happen, they would travel together. Then they were out of words. It was late. Eduardo took Janet's small white hand in his strong black one and led her toward their first floor bedroom with the big window facing the sea. The filmy curtains fluttered in the soft breeze that blew through the open window and the moon shed a narrow path of light across the bed.

In August they traveled to Geneva together, then Cairo, then London. Janet discovered that when she traveled with Eduardo, she took on something like a "first lady" status. Everywhere they went she was wined and dined and made to feel special. She liked the way her heart felt.

They worked well together on the road. She kept him organized, made sure he got to appointments on time, and kept detailed records of all his meetings as he shared them with her. They had come to a new level of understanding that made possible the strengthening of their relationship. He began to depend on her in ways he never had before. It filled her with a strange new bliss.

Chapter 19
"You Can't Mean It."

Janet watched as Frelimo's guerilla fighting strategy played out. The days lengthened and the temperature climbed. The small but growing band of fighters waged a series of hit-and-run, low-level encounters, gradually inching their way deeper into the Niassa and Cabo del Gado provinces of Mozambique that bordered Tanzania. The theory was that as they continued to accumulate small victories, the Portuguese would take notice and reconsider their commitment to keeping Mozambique under their domination. Frelimo had no idea how long this might take, but they were prepared for a long, slow fight.

"When we have control of about a third of the country, the Portuguese will give up," Eduardo predicted. He knew the winds of change that were blowing across Africa could not be stopped despite the best efforts of the Portuguese. French, British, and Belgian colonizers had already taken note and reluctantly granted their colonies independence. The Portuguese government was bucking an inevitable trend.

Eduardo's greatest challenge continued to be maintaining unity within Frelimo. The organization had emerged from the melding of three disparate organizations and its members struggled to work together, often battling for positions of power. Eduardo, always fighting tribalism and advocating a wider worldview, was accused by Party members of showing favoritism to those of his own tribe. His task was to keep the goal of independence from Portugal upmost in their thoughts and to calm their squabbles as best he could.

Yet, the war effort progressed. One by one, the fighters liberated small villages and the people rejoiced. As financial support for the Mozambique Institute grew thanks to Janet's fundraising efforts, she was able to send teams of workers into the liberated areas to begin setting up schools and health clinics. Two years into the war, by the end of 1966, the Mozambique Institute was operating 72 schools with an enrollment of 7,000 students. Her biggest challenge was staffing the schools with qualified teachers.

*****

Father Mateus Gwenjere, a former leader of an underground freedom movement in Lourenço Marques, managed to escape from the capital city and appeared in Dar to offer his services to the liberation front.

"He is important to our cause." Eduardo let Janet know how excited he was to have Gwenjere become active in the fight. He believed that Gwenjere would add strength to a delegation on its way to New York to tell their story to the United Nations and to plead for funding. Gwenjere went willingly, and while he was there he talked with Mozambican students studying in the U.S.

He listened to their concerns. "We don't think we should be forced to pay for our education by fighting for a year," the students told him.

"But you made a commitment when you came here to study, didn't you?" Gwenjere responded.

"Yes. That's true. But we feel that we have become too valuable to the cause to risk losing our lives fighting a guerilla war in the bush," their chosen spokesperson replied.

"You have a point there," Gwenjere said. "I'll support you in that." His encouragement had the result of strengthening an elitist attitude that grew among the students as they pursued their education.

When he returned from the U.S., Gwenjere set about inserting himself into the affairs of the Mozambican Institute. He was open about his disgust that the Institute was headed by a white American woman. Impassioned and persuasive, he lost no time in strenuously objecting to Frelimo's rule that Institute students take their turn in combat for a year. He was furious when Janet hired white teachers and allowed some classes to be taught in Portuguese, rather than English, calling Portuguese an "imperialistic" language.

"I wish I could hire black teachers, all fluent in English." Janet

114

tried to explain. "I can't find enough of them. You find me some qualified black teachers and I'll welcome them with open arms and pay
them well. Don't you understand? I have no choice. If I want teachers,
I have to hire whoever is available."

Gwenjere remained stubborn and unconvinced. 'There must be
qualified black teachers willing to come here. We must work harder to
find them," he responded.

Janet welcomed people from the ranks of Peace Corps volunteers
who were willing to teach. Sometimes the guerilla fighters took a turn
in the classroom as they waited for their military assignments. She persuaded a few Americans living in Tanzania to help out, but there were
never enough English teachers.

The discord that Gwenjere generated among Mozambican students
studying in the U.S. and among those in Tanzania eventually led to
acts of extended, horrific violence. Janet agonized as the atmosphere
became more and more poisonous. Fights and riots broke out. Students
and teachers suffered injuries as the violence grew. The existence of
the fledgling secondary school was in doubt. It was barely operating in
such a dangerous atmosphere.

A brief reprieve from her work and the pile of difficulties she was
confronting came when Janet returned to the U.S. for a hysterectomy.
"What a fine reason for a vacation," she quipped. In the hospital, she
was calm and pleased at the rest that had been forced upon her, chatting happily with the nurses. "This surgery is the only way I could
figure out how to get some time off." When they learned who she was
and what she was doing in Africa, they were full of questions. They
laughed when she thanked them for "liberating" her from an IV.

She was soon back in Dar where it was painfully evident to her
that her children had become victims of the revolution. Eddie, at age
eleven, was now old enough to understand the dangers he and his
family were facing. For a couple of days after Janet's return, Eddie
remained inconsolable. "Come here," Janet called to him, reaching out
for a hug. "Why so sad?"

"One night while you were away, we had to sleep across town with
the Sullivans. Dad didn't tell me anything, but I heard the grown-ups

talking. Someone said they were going to kill us all. I don't want to stay here any more."

Janet held him tight. "I promise you will be safe," she whispered. "We will always make sure that you are safe. Promise." She only wished that she could totally believe the words she said to him with such certainty.

As the war intensified, Janet approached Eduardo. "As much as I love to travel with you, I don't think we should go away together for a while. It's too hard on the children. And if something happened and we both disappeared, it would be so much worse for them."

Just back from the fighting front and preparing for yet another fundraising trip to Europe, Eduardo agreed with her. "I've been thinking the same thing. That's the way it has to be for now."

Janet was torn between two commitments; to her young children and to the dream of independence she shared with Eduardo. "I think raising these children the way we are doing and the way we must, is likely to be the greatest challenge of our lives." Eduardo nodded his head and took her into his arms.

*****

Eduardo had reached a breaking point. "Our efforts here are useless. Let's give up this fight and go back to the U.S. where we can raise our children in safety and make a good living." He'd been seeking funding to keep the war going, making regular trips to the fighting front, dealing with power struggles in Frelimo and confronting Gwenjere's outspoken objection to Janet as head of the Mozambican Institute. It all became too much.

"Quit? Give up? You can't mean it. Our work here is not done. You need a few days in Switzerland. Go see Jean-Paul." Janet kept working, suffering through month after month of violence. Gwenjere instigated crisis after crisis. Three white teachers and the white doctor at the health clinic in Dar es Salaam were harassed and left the country. An attack on the Frelimo offices caused a beating so severe that the recipient of the violence, a beloved teacher, died after a month of agony in the hospital.

Gradually Janet came to understand some of the reasons for the bubbling discontent that eventually resulted in the need to close the secondary school. Black consciousness was on the rise everywhere causing radical anti-white feelings. The Catholic Church did not support independence fearing that they would lose power in an independent Mozambique. Frelimo members who disagreed with Eduardo did what they could to make his life difficult. Janet remained resolute through it all. In a letter to her parents when the worst seemed to be over, she wrote, "I think I am now wiser, stronger and I know that I am more determined than ever to see this endeavor to its conclusion."

Chapter 20
"I Will Take a Hot Bath"

In July 1968, the second congress of the Frelimo party met in the newly liberated province of Niassa. Janet was relieved when Eduardo was elected president for a second four-year term. She listened with pride as he responded to the confidence placed in him by Party members. He praised his fellow Mozambicans, men and a few women, from different tribes and religious groups, who came together despite their differences for a greater goal—securing independence for their country.

"Progress may seem slow sometimes but we have come a long way in the last four years," Eduardo said, addressing the gathering. "Many villages in the northern provinces are now free from Portuguese control, and people are beginning to rebuild their lives. We are working to reassure them by building schools and health clinics in the villages as quickly as we can. Keep the faith. This war won't last forever."

*****

In November, Janet set off alone on an extended fundraising tour of Europe. She solicited funds for the Mozambican Institute in Holland, Scandinavia, Britain and several Eastern European countries. Pleased with her success, she shared her thoughts with Eduardo. At the age of thirty-four, she was coming into her own as a savvy fundraiser. "It's not until I begin talking that people take me seriously. When they look at me, I get the feeling that they see me as a cute little American girl and have a lot of trouble connecting me to the liberation struggle. They seem to take me more seriously when they realize that I have something to say to them."

The response she received from countries who expressed their solidarity with the liberation effort and made donations to the humanitarian work of the Institute brought her great satisfaction. At last Frelimo was gaining a reputation as a legitimate movement with high standards. The world had begun to understand that the painfully slow guerilla war Frelimo was waging was showing results. She was careful to explain that the Institute was not involved with the fighting. Only after a village became free, did the Institute move in to establish schools and health clinics, a tangible way to let the citizens know that with the coming of independence their lives were about to become better.

At home, Eduardo reported that twelve-year-old Eddie was thriving in his military training, often doing better than boys older than he. He was also becoming fluent in Portuguese. Eduardo suggested to Janet that it might be time to begin using Portuguese as their family language. He closed his letter saying, "The perfect thing we had just before you left is being nursed in my spirit all the time, so that I may keep myself warm inside for as long as you have to be away."

Janet treated herself to Christmas in the U.S. with her parents, siblings and their families. Then she flew to London where she enrolled in an intensive two-week course to upgrade her fluency in Portuguese. When the class finished, she headed to Switzerland for a few days of rest before returning to Mozambique.

She arrived in Geneva tired but satisfied that she had accomplished what she had set out to do on her long trip. She settled into a small apartment owned by Jean- Paul Widmer. It was early evening. Janet kicked off her shoes, poured herself a glass of wine and relaxed into the deep cushions of a comfortable old couch, the only furniture in the tiny living room.

Moments later a sharp knock on her door roused her. Jean-Paul appeared accompanied by a man she did not know wearing a clerical collar. As Janet rose to greet Jean-Paul, he took her into his outstretched arms. "Eduardo's had a accident," he said, holding her tight. Pulling away from him so that she could look into his eyes, she asked, "Has Eduardo been hurt?"

No answer. "Has he been badly hurt?"

No answer. "He's dead, isn't he?"

"Yes. Eduardo died."

The man in the clerical collar asked, "Would you like to pray?
    "No. I will take a hot bath."

Chapter 21
Like a Festival

In the morning, Janet went shopping. She bought a cream-colored dress for herself and pink frocks for Chude and Nyeleti. "I refuse to sink into a black mourning hole," she told the friend who went with her. "I won't have the Portuguese crowing over me, watching me suffer. I will continue to function. I will continue to fight."

Communication between Switzerland and Tanzania was so sporadic and difficult that Janet knew few details about what happened. She was told that her three children were safe and cared for, and that put her mind at ease. Jean-Paul accompanied her on the flight to Dar es Salaam.

Knowing who was behind the assassination of Eduardo was not a high priority for Janet. She suspected the Portuguese Secret Police who had been watching them closely for a long time. They had identified Eduardo as a prime mover in the fight for independence and had been biding their time, waiting for an opportunity to get rid of him.

Eduardo sat down at his desk on the morning of February 3, 1969 after returning from the fighting front, anticipating a day of paperwork. As Janet heard the story, she could imagine how he must have been feeling. He much preferred action, but perhaps, given the circumstances, a quiet day at his desk, out of the heat and humidity, might have had some appeal for him just then.   The mail came early. Spotting a book-size package, he plucked it from the top of the pile and began to tear away the brown paper wrapping. In moments it blew up in his hands with a deafening roar that brought three people running to him from adjacent offices. The blast was powerful enough that it killed him instantly, exploding into his chest and enveloping his office in smoke, flame and bits of debris.

Interpol and the Tanzanian police eventually concluded that the bomb had been built in Beira, a coastal city in Mozambique, probably by the Portuguese Secret Police. Investigators believed the bomb might have been carried to Tanzania by an individual who had attempted to form a separatist movement within Frelimo and then tried to persuade the Tanzanian government to close the border with Mozambique to Frelimo fighters. A month earlier he had been released from Frelimo because of these actions. None of this mattered much to Janet.

Uria Simango, a Congregational minister and vice president of Frelimo who had twice lost to Eduardo in a vote for the presidency, also came under suspicion. He deserted the Party shortly after Eduardo's death but years later, in 1974, rejoined the Party in a vain attempt to seize power. The following year he admitted to helping transport the bomb that killed Eduardo. After independence he was imprisoned in Mozambique where he eventually died.

"Answers won't bring Eduardo back," Janet told the investigators. "Revenge is not part of my make-up. Eduardo was killed because of the work he was doing. That's enough for me. He continued the effort to liberate his country with the knowledge that he was likely to be killed for doing what he believed he had to do."

American William Minter and his wife Ruth had spent two years teaching in Mozambique Institute schools. When their time was up, Eduardo said good-bye to them at the airport on New Year's Day, 1969. Minter wrote about Eduardo in a chapter of *No Easy Victories, African Liberation and American Activists over a Half Century 1950-2000*, a book he edited. In the chapter he wrote, "Unfinished Journeys," he said: "Had he (Eduardo) lived to see the freedom of his country, he would likely have joined his contemporary and friend, Nelson Mandela, as one of Africa's most respected leaders. I was one of many inspired by his leadership. His sacrifice reinforced our commitments. The deaths of Mondlane and others involved in freedom movements had profound impact not only in their own countries, but around the world."

Janet was overwhelmed by all the people who came to offer their sympathy and support. Not for a moment was she was allowed to disappear into a corner to grieve in private. A few days after Jean-Paul returned to Switzerland, she wrote to him to explain her decision to stay in Tanzania and continue the fight. She was just beginning to comprehend the enormous scope of the role she had been left to fill.

When Samora Machel, then in charge of the fighting force, and his men, engaged in combat deep in northern Mozambique, learned of Eduardo's death, they were so stunned that they were unable to move. After two days, when they received word that Janet had decided to stay in Dar and continue her work, they found the strength to begin the long trek back to headquarters. All along the way they spread the word that Janet was staying in the fight, leaving behind them a trail of determination and solidarity among the people.

Dignitaries from around the world came for Eduardo's service. Uria Simango, not yet suspected of having a role in Eduardo's death, preached a sermon. Ed Hawley, Eduardo's friend from Oberlin days who had married Eduardo and Janet in his living room, spoke as well.

Janet's determination to stay in the fight gave everyone the courage to continue. It was as if she had become national property. Her life was no longer her own. There were times when she was gripped by fear of what the future might hold, but she kept those qualms to herself.

Inside she ached with the loss of her love, the man who had been the central focus of her life for seventeen years. She worried that she would falter, that she would fall apart and disappoint the whole community counting on her to stay strong. These thoughts haunted her dreams through periods of fitful sleep and awakened her through long, lonely nights.

During the day, the Mondlane home overflowed with visitors. In the African tradition, a widow belongs to the family of her husband. The members of Frelimo saw Janet and her children as their family. She belonged to them and they came to offer comfort and support. "It was a blessing for the children to have so many kind people around," Janet wrote to Jean-Paul. "From the outside, our house looks like we're having some sort of grand festival."

Libby James

Chapter 22
Surrounded With Love

A few days before Eduardo was killed, Chude had a dream. In it she watched her father hurtle over a cliff, thrown from the car he was riding in before it rolled on top of him. So it was that the day when an unfamiliar face driving the family car arrived to retrieve Chude and Eddie from school, that Chude's antenna went up.

"Something's happened to Dad." Chude grabbed Eddie's arm as they drove off. "I know something terrible has happened to him."

"How do you know? Don't jump to conclusions." Eddie stared straight ahead and without another word, moved closer to his sister in the back seat of the car. They rode the rest of the way in silence until they arrived at the home of Marcelino Dos Santos, vice president of Frelimo. Marcelino's wife, Pam, met them in the driveway, tears streaming down her face. She walked them to a nearby park, sat them down on a bench and told them that their father was dead.

When she led them back to her house, she laid two tranquilizers on the kitchen table and told Eddie and Chude the pills would make them feel better. "Your father died in an explosion. No one knows who caused it. Nyeleti will be here soon. You two must be brave. Promise me you will not tell her. She is so young. We must wait and let your mother do that."

Eddie swallowed the tranquilizer and soon fell asleep, but Chude felt an urgent need to run outside and scream. She had to talk to someone. She helped herself to a bicycle and pedaled to the home of her friend, Becky Hawley. "My dad has been killed. My best friend. The only one who really understood me." At the news, Becky fell silent and turned her head away. Chude felt utterly alone.

"Where's my dad?" Nyeleti asked the strange man driving the family's car who had come to pick her up from school. Eduardo always picked her up when he was at home. The stranger said he didn't know. Instead of driving Nyeleti home, he dropped her off at the Dos Santos home. Chude and Eddie were already there, sitting silent at the kitchen table, tear-stained and solemn.

"Where's dad?" They didn't answer her. Nyeleti was confused. *Why were Eddie and Chude so quiet? Why were they at the Dos Santos' house when they should be at home and why was she there as well?* No one answered her questions. She had to have known that something momentous had happened but no one told her anything. Everyone seemed very sad and would not talk to her. Her father had disappeared. She was told nothing until her mother arrived home two days later. Nyeleti was by nature a quiet child and did not press for answers to her questions.

The three children greeted Janet on her arrival, thankful to be back in their own home. The Dos Santos family had done their best to care for them until Janet returned and for that Janet was forever grateful. She struggled to find the words to explain to Nyeleti what had happened, all the time knowing that there were none. "Daddy died fighting for his country, Nyeleti. He knew this might happen but he was very brave and kept on doing his work."

Nyeleti clung to her, sobbing. "Why would anyone want to kill Dad when he was so good and kind? I don't understand, Mom. What are we going to do?"

*****

In the days to come, Janet found it difficult to offer comfort to Chude. "Be strong. We all have to be strong." Chude gave her a blank look and escaped to her room. Janet cried. When they met in the kitchen a little later, she took Chude in her arms but found she could not hold her for more than a few seconds. "I'm not abandoning you, Chude. I love you. It's just that for right now, this is the only way I can be. Both of us have to get through this whatever way we can."

Janet knew how Chude had idolized her father. She knew that this girl needed someone other than her mother to talk to about her loss. Eduardo had been her biggest supporter; the one who played with her, encouraged her talent for singing and dancing, and could sense what was churning inside her head. Chude needed more attention and more permission to grieve her loss than anyone around her was able to give her at the time.

"My Dad loved that hat," Chude grabbed it when Eduardo's things were being cleared out of the house. "Please, don't give it away." She felt the same about his bow ties, remembering how much he liked to get dressed up. Seeing these things disappear, things that had been so much a part of her father, added to her sense of loss.

It was the gentle Josina Muthemba, who would eventually be able to get through to Chude and make her feel safe. At Janet's invitation, Josina came to live with the Mondlanes after Eduardo's death. When Janet saw Chude and Josina bonding, she felt relieved and grateful. Josina had been living across town and had recently become engaged to Samora Machel.

After getting to know the Mondlanes in Jao Belo on their trip around Mozambique years before, Josina and her uncle, Matheus Muthemba, had moved to Tanzania to join the war effort. Josina had put aside her studies to focus on the liberation effort, and at times saw combat, moving beyond the supporting role usually filled by the women fighters. She had lost a fiancé in the fighting at the beginning of the war. Samora, her new love, was away most of the time serving as the military leader of the fighting front in northern Mozambique. Before Janet left on her trip in November, Samora had given her money to buy wedding rings when she was in Switzerland.

After Eduardo's death, Josina slept in Janet's bedroom with her. Janet could not bear to be alone at night. Josina was quiet and did not share her thoughts freely and easily. She was like Janet in this way. She didn't say much and Janet didn't want her to. It was her calming presence that was important to Janet during the first painful weeks after Eduardo's death.

One day Eddie opened a big brown envelope that arrived in the mail to find a book with a note inside. "This time it isn't a bomb. We just want you to know that we haven't forgotten you," it read. There was so much tension in the air everywhere she went that Janet decided

to try to get her children out of Dar es Salaam for a time.   When Janet left her house, to go to her office or into town, she did not feel safe.
People looked at her in strange ways, at least she thought they did.
Wherever she went, the mood seemed heavy and joyless. She heard no
chatter or laughter in the streets. She fell into a state of anxiety, worrying about the safety of her children.

Despite the troubling times and her worries about her children,
Janet never reconsidered her decision to stay in Dar. In the first days
after Eduardo's death and for the months to come, it was her work with
the Institute that helped to maintain her sanity.

A few weeks after Eduardo's death, colleagues asked Janet if she'd
be willing to make a trip by foot into the liberated area in northern Mozambique. The people would welcome her, they said. She could assure
them of her loyalty and her commitment to continuing the struggle.

"The trip will do you good. "I'll go with you," Josina said. "You'll
see just how important you are to the people. It will be wonderful for
you to see the schools and clinics that your fundraising and recruiting
efforts have created. You'll be inspired to keep on."

Janet hesitated about taking the trip. It would be physically strenu-
ous and it involved some risk. If the Portuguese captured her, it would
be a real coup for their side. There would be days of walking through
wooded, hilly territory. Weeks of tension and grieving had left Janet
drained, exhausted and thinner. But in the end, she decided to go.

She knew enough to wear broken-in hiking boots, but Josina, who
agreed to accompany her, suffered in new boots that caused painful
blisters. Janet produced some gauze and tape from her backpack and
shared them with Josina. "Maybe this will help. You're just going to
have to make the best of it."

With only a little help from a fellow traveler who volunteered to
carry her backpack over the mountain near the border between Tanzania and Mozambique, Janet made the climb over loose rock without a
problem. In addition to being weak from weight loss, she had a stubborn case of diarrhea when the trip began, but she kept that information to herself.

When the little group of travelers pulled into a base camp, they

130

were expected to give a presentation to the village people. Words and gestures of love and appreciation flowed from these villagers who were benefitting from the liberation effort. They were delighted to meet Janet and hear her words of encouragement. "We're making progress," she told them. "Be patient. The day will come when you will be a citizen of a free country with all the rights and privileges that come with that status."

The armed conflict became real to Janet when a helicopter streaked across the sky as she was speaking to a group of villagers. "I am as determined as you are to stay in this fight until all our efforts are rewarded with independence, no matter how many years it takes." Cheers rose in response to her words.

The sound was loud enough to drown out her closing words. As the Portuguese helicopter circled and swooped low to make their presence known, Janet clutched her shiny white briefcase with its two little handles and stood as if cemented to the ground. She experienced a bizarre, otherworldly moment when she wondered how she came to be here, perhaps the target of an attack, in a remote village in the bush of northern Mozambique.

"Take cover," a scruffy young guerilla shouted, waving his arms to get the group of visitors moving. "We'll finish our meeting later. And hide that briefcase, Mama, before it becomes a target for our visitors from the sky."

Everyone scattered. Janet stuffed her briefcase into her shirt and followed Josina into the meager cover of the dusty mopane bushes at the outskirts of the village. They'd been shown an air raid shelter earlier in the day, a hole in the ground really, but Janet wasn't sure why, because they were also warned to stay away from it should there be an aerial attack. When a helicopter landed, anyone who'd taken cover in the shelter was a sitting duck, perched in a dark hole with no escape from the drawn AK47's of the Portuguese.

Janet winced as she saw Josina hobbling, stumbling in pain as she ran for cover. Huddled together with a half dozen villagers and a few guerillas who did their best to reassure and protect them, Janet and Josina stayed close to each other and waited in silence until the helicopters flew off.

The villagers knew that their country would not be quickly or easily wrested from the grip of 500 years of Portuguese domination. Over time they had learned to be patient. When Janet saw the dedication of the people she met as she traveled, her determination to achieve the goal that she and Eduardo had clung to for so many years took on new importance and grew stronger.

Food became a big issue on the trip. The group was burning many calories as they trekked. They ate cassava, sweet potatoes and occasionally were treated to chicken in the villages they visited, in acknowledgement of their high status. They drank Johnson's Lipton Tea, made from a powder mixed with boiling water. "This is a delicious drink." Janet said appreciating its warmth and sweetness. "Maybe I like it so much because my name was Johnson before I married."

Janet had begun this unlikely journey from Tanzania weak and thin from grief. But as the days passed, she began to feel stronger. The first few mornings of the trip she awakened with every muscle in her body screaming from hours of tramping through rough terrain and nights spent on a dirt floor with a blanket wrapped around her or on a crude cot made from sticks. As she slowly adjusted, the long hours of exercise began to pay off. She had never walked so far in her life. The long days of trekking agreed with her and raised her spirits. On the way home, at a camp near the border, Janet eased off her boots and began to rub her aching feet. One of the women militia sat down beside her. "You know, you have the most beautiful feet," she said looking longingly at Janet's pink and white toes.

"Thank you." Janet smiled. She felt a little embarrassed. Here was a woman whose life had been spent carrying heavy loads, often barefoot. Her feet were crusted and looked as if they had seldom been enclosed in anything more than sandals fashioned from old tires. *Of course she wished for pretty feet. And I come along with my smooth feet, sore, yes, but soft and free of crusty callouses.* She was touched by the woman's words of genuine longing.

It was to be Janet's only trip into the war zone. The Tanzanians began restricting all non-military people from going into southern Tanzania and beyond, supposedly because of heavy fighting in the area. This trip would be her only opportunity to visit the schools and clinics she had helped to establish in the liberated areas. She had hoped to return to nurture relationships with teachers and medical staff in the schools and medical clinics, making it easier to assess needs and monitor expenditures.

Janet returned to Dar with a head full of ideas and the mental and physical stamina to begin implementing them. The first thing she did was set the wheels in motion to re-open the Mozambique Institute secondary school that had been closed for nearly two years.

In a letter to Jean-Paul, she shared her new state of mind:

"Our lives have begun to steady themselves. We keep Eduardo close to us, talk about him. Laugh about the funny things he said and remember the way he did things. Slowly, we realize that he is not going to do these things for us and that we are going to have to do them for ourselves. We have been trying to keep the happiness that was Eduardo and at the same time know that our happiness will now have to come from within ourselves.

"We have accepted his physical loss in our midst, yet have found a place for him among us where he will stay and help us in much the same way as before. I could never understand the tradition of feasting after the death of someone so beloved, but now I understand it very well. The children have found themselves surrounded with love. No doubt they will feel loneliness in the future, but they can never reach despair because it has been made so clear to them that their sorrows and their joys are melded with many others who love them dearly."

Libby James

Chapter 23
Going It alone

❝Women don't choose to become prostitutes, but a family's empty stomachs can be the mother of desperation." Janet didn't soft pedal her comments as she described the struggle of Mozambican women under Portuguese rule at a women's conference in Helsinki, Finland. She explained that the current economic system encouraged an apartheid-like atmosphere designed to deny the black native population equal rights with the white colonizers. Prostitution was not against the law. In fact, the Portuguese government saw it as a legitimate way to make a living. Only four percent of the national budget was allotted for education. The literacy rate hovered at around two percent. It was no wonder career options for women were severely limited. "When women are ignorant, they are powerless and a nation is weak," Janet said.

"In 1964, when we came to the sad realization that there was no way to achieve independence without resorting to violence, the Frelimo Party began, with 250 fighters, to initiate guerilla war. We took the Portuguese by surprise with a single night-time attack on an outpost in the north, close to the border with Tanzania. Today we have 10,000 well-equipped, trained fighters moving slowly but steadily against 60,000 Portuguese troops. And now Portugal is spending fifty percent of its budget on what they call 'defense.' Translate that as making war on our freedom fighters. "

Josina attended the conference with Janet and shared stories about the women who had become an important part of the struggle for independence, fighting alongside the men and devoting their minds, bodies and spirits to the cause of independence. Josina had postponed her schooling to join the cause. "We women do more than support our freedom fighters," she told the women at the conference. "We produce our food and care for our families. We nurse the victims of war, including children. We work in health units. When we must, we carry weapons and join combat units. When an area is liberated, we move in to help build schools and clinics in the villages. Little by little, we are making progress. We know victory is not likely to come soon but we are committed to what we are doing. It is a life and death struggle."

During these days, Janet devoted herself to the task of soliciting funds to keep the Mozambique Institute alive and growing. She traveled to Europe frequently where she met with loyal supporters and sought out new ones. A critical part of her work was to foster the development of solidarity groups with the capacity to provide on-going support for the Institute.

Josina continued to live in the Mondlane household, developing an ever closer friendship with Janet. She turned to Janet for advice as she made plans to marry Samora. He was away at the Front, in charge of Frelimo's military operation, and could only manage occasional short visits to Dar.

After one of his trips, Josina consulted with Janet. "Samora has asked if I'd be willing to marry him at military headquarters in Tunduru. He can't take the time to come to Dar to get married right now. What do you think?"

"I think we need to make a plan to go to Tunduru. "I wouldn't miss your wedding for the world."

The trip to military headquarters deep in southern Tanzania, meant hours of travel across nearly impassable dirt roads scarred with ruts, rocks, and potholes. When they arrived, exhausted and covered with road dirt, they discovered that there was no place for Janet to stay. She ended up spending the couple's wedding night with them in a mud hut.

"Sorry," Josina told Janet the next morning. "Did we keep you awake last night?"

"Never mind," Janet replied giving her a knowing smile.

When Samora was able to escape from the Front for a few days, he joined Josina in the Mondlane home. It wasn't long before Josina was expecting a child.

Josina, Janet and the children liked to spend summer evenings at a local drive-in movie, often inviting some of the fighters in town on leave to join them in their VW van. Drinks, snacks and laughter allowed them to forget the realities of war for a few hours. Everyone loved the diversion provided by a silly movie.

One night, halfway through *Pink Panther*, Josina began to squirm. "I'm feeling um--kind of funny," she whispered to Janet. "It's my stomach."

Her due date was close enough that Janet did not hesitate. Above the loud objections of the children, she quickly returned the speaker to its post and roared out of the drive-in halfway through the movie, headed for the hospital. "We're not taking any chances," she announced. "There's no stopping a baby when it decides it's time to come into the world."

By the next morning, little Samito had arrived. There had been no time for Samora to get to Dar for the birth.

Janet and the children found little Samito a source of great joy in their household. Chude took a special interest in the little boy, holding and rocking him every time she had a chance. When he cried, she sang to him and her sweet voice never failed to calm him. "Someday you will be a wonderful mother," Josina told Chude. "Look at the way he's smiling. You have a special touch."

As the days went by, Janet noticed that Josina seemed to tire easily and had very little energy. At first she thought it was because of the sleepless nights that go along with having a newborn. When she asked Josina how she was feeling, she would only say that it was taking her longer than she'd thought it should for her to recover from childbirth. "I have this nagging pain in my stomach," she admitted to Janet. "I wonder what that's all about."

"Something's not right. You'd better get checked out." Janet made her a doctor's appointment. The local doctors were puzzled. When they were unable to find the source of her trouble, Janet suggested that Josina seek advice in Russia. At the time, Frelimo had a close relationship with the Soviet Union, so it seemed the logical place to go. Janet knew that good medical care was available there.

Josina agreed to make the trip, leaving Samito in the care of the

Mondlanes. In two weeks, when she came home, she said little and seemed distant--even distraught at times, Janet thought. But she did not pry. Josina said only, "I'm the unluckiest girl in the world."

*****

Only a few months later, Janet was at a conference in Holland when she received a garbled telegram in Portuguese that she could barely decipher. She finally figured out that the words described the sudden death of Josina from an undetermined illness. Details were few. Far from home, alone in a hotel room, Janet's first reaction was denial. She refused to believe the words she had just read. When reality finally sank in, she collapsed.

"I simply lost it. For the weeks and months following Eduardo's death, I had been able to hold it together, but the shock of Josina's untimely death at such a young age was more than I could handle. I flung myself on the bed, buried my head in the pillow and just let loose," she wrote to her mother. "Josina's death undid me."

But there was no time for Janet to indulge in an extended meltdown. She forced herself to keep on with her work, spearheading the effort to maintain the flow of funds to the Mozambique Institute. She had become comfortable requesting funds. She never hesitated to ask, and she was finding ways to make it hard for those she approached to tell her no. Her skills were growing and her reputation as a skilled fundraiser was growing.

*****

As she negotiated her way through her new circumstances as a single white woman living in Africa with her three biracial children, Janet recalled her visit to Mozambique in 1960. She had arrived with two toddlers, determined to absorb all she could of the ways of this place, so strange and new to her. The people she met were kind but she felt confused by cultural differences and by the racist attitudes she encountered among the missionaries. When Eduardo joined her, life was suddenly easier. She realized now that it was his presence and his subtle guidance that made her feel comfortable, that taught her to ignore small injustices and save her energy for issues that were important. He insulated her from the awkwardness of being a white woman trying to find her way in the country of the black man she'd married.

No longer the wife of Frelimo's president, Janet found her world had changed. Her status as Eduardo's widow made her a revered symbol of the movement but at the same time, as a white woman alone in a black country, she was learning that her influence had its limits.

Some loyal Frelimo Party members saw her as an interloper, a white woman who had married a black man and for some reason, unfathomable to them, had become passionate about the Mozambican struggle for independence. Even those closest to her could not understand how she could be as dedicated as she was to their cause. Africans' strong allegiance to their own tribes made it impossible for most of them to conceive of the depth of her desire to achieve independence for people who were not of her own race. The Mozambican community in Dar was surprised that after Eduardo's death Janet did not take her American-born children and go home to her family.

Even though he had been away frequently when they were in Tanzania, Eduardo's status had continued to provide an invisible shield for Janet. Now the shield was gone. Resentment of her whiteness came bubbling to the surface. She encountered unexpected barriers in her work. The Tanzanians made it obvious that they resented her white presence. The support they had once shown for the Mozambican Institute diminished. They refused to allow her to travel across the border, saying they feared for her safety. They chafed at dealing with a white woman in a position of power in a time when they were fighting for their independence from white colonizers, regardless of the good work she was doing.

Janet recorded her thoughts and reactions in letters to her mother. "It feels like I'm running headfirst into rushing waters in a strange new territory, and I'm not at all sure how things will end up. I'm learning not to worry about whether I am American or Mozambican or whether I will ever be able to assimilate into the society where I find myself. I have decided that I can only function as the person I have always been. I cannot hesitate to speak out and I cannot be fearful of what other people may think of me. I am determined to move ahead with what I believe to be the right path for me."

Libby James

Chapter 24
The Children

❝I see raising these three children of ours as the greatest challenge of my life." Eduardo had smiled at Janet's words spoken long ago. He reminded her that the challenge was his as much as it was hers. She recalled his words as she confronted the parenting responsibility that was now hers alone. Following Eduardo's assassination in early 1969, the atmosphere of fear that arose in Dar es Salaam frightened Janet, not so much for herself, but for her children. She wished that for a while at least, she could find them safer places to live. She had been thinking these thoughts for months. They refused to go away.

Their parents' political involvement had always determined where the Mondlane children lived, where they went to school, who became their friends, where they traveled, the dangers they faced, their outlook on the world and the opportunities they were denied or presented with.

The children sacrificed for a cause they could not possibly, especially when they were very young, understand or believe in. Eduardo and Janet often talked about the effect their commitments and lifestyle were likely to have on their children. They worried about keeping them safe. But they were on a path they could not change.

"Eduardo and I have the luxury of choosing what we plan to do," Janet told her sister when she was preparing to pack up her children and leave the U.S. for a browbeaten stretch of sub-Saharan territory. "Our children have to go along. They have no choice—they have no control over their destinies."

Eddie had already spent a summer at a camp in East Germany and Janet hoped he would be able to return there in the summer of 1969. When she learned that there was no space for him at the camp, she re-

141

signed herself to keeping him at home. At the age of seven, there was nowhere for Nyeleti to go, and while she feared for Nyeleti's safety, Janet was torn because she realized that her youngest child needed to be at home with her, in familiar territory.

Before Eduardo's death, he and Janet had been looking for a school for Chude that would allow her to develop her talent for singing and dancing. Their old friend, Herb Shore, now living in Philadelphia, suggested a performance academy in the city that he thought would be a good school for Chude. Now seemed the right time to take him up on his offer. Chude could live with the Shore family, enroll in the school and pursue her passion for voice and dance.

Taking Eddie and Nyeleti along with her, Janet delivered a teary-eyed eleven-year-old Chude to Philadelphia, cautioning her to be strong and to be in touch when she had good news to report. *I was protecting myself from hearing about her sadness. I was just barely dealing with my own*, she reflected after she parted from her daughter.

The time she spent in Philadelphia was a roller-coaster experience for Chude. When Herb Shore had a heart attack, she was no longer able to stay with his family. From then on, she bounced from one family to another, never staying in one place long enough to feel settled.

When she had learned all she could at the academy, she returned to Dar es Salaam and enrolled in military training close by as her brother had done before her. Afterwards, with Janet's blessing, she went to Moscow, hoping to study at the Bolshoi Ballet School. By this time Eddie was studying at an international school in Ivanova in the Soviet Union.

"Racism," Chude concluded when the Bolshoi School refused to admit her, explaining that she was "the wrong shape" for a dancer. She enrolled in another school in the Soviet Union where she was able to continue her studies in dance and voice.

Eddie's experience at school in Ivanova was not a happy one. He had been accustomed to an academic atmosphere at the international school in Dar where individuals were respected and critical thinking was encouraged. He was uncomfortable with the rigidity of the school in Ivanova. Learning was largely rote memorization, with little or no opportunity for back and forth discussion. The school tried to make him join the student socialist movement. He refused. Things did not go well for Eddie after that. Back home in Dar, he confided to his mother. "When Samora came to visit me, one of my teachers made me promise not to tell him about the physical punishment that happened all the time at school."

"Were you ever hit? Janet was shocked to hear what Eddie had to say.

"Well yes, but everyone was. We got used to it. When Samora was there, he took me aside. 'The quickest way to turn someone into a capitalist is to send them to the Soviet Union.' That's what he told me."

"But mom, I want to stay at home. I can go to school right here and be close to you." Janet had decided Nyeleti would be safer if she left Dar to attend the Frelimo primary boarding school in Bagamoyo, about an hour from home. She was one of the youngest at the school and had never lived away from home before. She didn't speak any of the languages used at the school. The food was strange. The children of Frelimo Party members who attended the school had been separated from their parents for years. "They don't even know what homesick means, mom."

Yet slowly Nyeleti began to adapt to her new surroundings. When she came home on breaks, Janet noticed changes. "Nyeleti, do they make you wear a headscarf in class?"

"You feel pretty weird if you don't when everyone else has one on."

She didn't look her mother in the eye the way she used to do when they spoke to each other. "Look at me when I'm talking to you." Nyeleti kept her eyes lowered. When she spoke, Janet noticed that she had picked up a singsong intonation in her voice.

Nyeleti felt exhausted all the time at school. She had trouble staying awake in class and often fell asleep before she finished her homework at night. She had no appetite.

"What's the matter with you?" a teacher asked her one day. "You must pay attention in class if you expect to learn anything here." Nothing changed. "Are you pretending to be ill so that we will send you home?" Nyeleti just looked at her teacher and said nothing.

It was the school's director who finally realized that there was something seriously wrong with Nyeleti. She sent her home. Nyeleti was happy to be home but didn't feel well enough to do anything but lie on the couch all day. "This girl has a serious form of malaria. I'm not sure we can treat it here," the doctor in Dar told Janet. He suggested that Nyeleti might benefit from going abroad for treatment.

Janet was so deeply involved in her work with the Institute that she made the decision to send Nyeleti to Switzerland alone where she knew Jean Paul-Widmer would come to her aid as he had done in the past. She put her young daughter on a plane and counted on the kindness of a flight attendant to make sure that she reached her destination safely and was met by Jean-Paul. He retrieved a sick, frightened little girl from the airport. He wasn't at all sure what to do to help her. After setting up a medical appointment for her, he contacted some friends and prevailed upon them to take her into their home high in the mountains where it was felt that the air would be beneficial. The family was kind and nurturing and found Nyeleti the treatment she needed to recover.

Years later Chude didn't hesitate to acknowledge difficult times during her growing up years, especially after her father's death, but she was able to look back and describe the extraordinary gift her parents had given her.

"I cannot be more grateful that I lived with those two people. When I first discovered racism, I was shocked by it…not even shocked really…I thought of it as ignorance, that's what they taught me. They both did that. I think perhaps more my mother than my father, because he didn't have much time. She gave me a lot of that. Maybe that is my downfall as well because I see life as they taught me, which is that everyone has something to do in life and they must do it…everybody is born with talents regardless of color and economic standards, that is the number one thing my parents taught me.

"They didn't have problems because of their different cultures. She was so much in love and he was so happy to have her. That was their security. There was nothing secure about their lives, so I think that their love for each other was was the one secure thing we children had…"

Chapter 25
Back in Maputo

Mozambique's decade-long struggle for independence ended abruptly with a whimper. No great battle or negotiations marked the victory. Instead a coup in Portugal brought a new regime into power. Beset as the Portuguese government was by the high cost of wars they were waging in Angola and Mozambique, they simply gave up and went away. In June 1975, Mozambique officially became a free and independent nation.

"It got too expensive to fight and the war was over, just like that." Janet cabled home with the news.

She spent her last days in Tanzania closing down the Mozambique Institute and packing for the move to Maputo, Mozambique's renamed capital city. She found the work a bittersweet endeavor. She had to leave Eduardo's remains behind and say good-bye to colleagues and friends who had supported each other through one crisis after another. None of it was easy.

Samora Machel, successor to Eduardo as president of Frelimo and now the new president of independent Mozambique, embarked on a triumphal march from the north into the capitol city. He and his entourage were cheered by joyous well-wishers all along the way. Janet was not included in the entourage. Samora paused on his way to pick up Nyeleti, now 13, who was at a camp in northern Mozambique. She was happy to join the procession and to be with Samito, who was like a brother to her. Samora's arrival in Maputo was greeted with high-flying flags, and streets lined with bands and cheering crowds. A new era was beginning. The people were filled with hope.

Journalist Robin Wright interviewed Janet before she left Dar and wrote an article in which she described her as "godmother to a revolution," a description so fitting that it stuck. Eddie and Chude returned from studies in the Soviet Union to join Janet for the trip to Maputo. They were toddlers clinging to their 25-year-old mother when they first set foot in Mozambique in 1960. As young adults, they made their second trip to the country that was to become their home under far different circumstances.

The plane from Dar carrying Janet, Chude and Eddie landed at the Maputo airport. The three of them stepped off the plane unnoticed. Unlike the day 15 years ago when they arrived for the first time, this time no one was there to greet them. No bands, no flags, not even a friendly face appeared to welcome them home. Customs and immigration officials did not react to their names when they stamped passports and ushered them through the arrival formalities.

Now her journey was done. Janet felt exhaustion taking over. "It is a little strange there's no one at all here to welcome us. They're probably busy. Maybe they forgot that I'm their godmother," she quipped. Samora had promised that Janet and her family would be provided with a place to live in Maputo. She hailed a taxi and handed the driver the address she'd been given.

After a 20-minute ride through streets teeming with people, buses, taxis, bicycles and a few animals, lined on either side with stalls selling everything from fruit to furniture, the threesome arrived at a shabby apartment building in the center of town. A note with Janet's name on it taped to the front door explained in English that an apartment on the fourth floor was to be their temporary quarters.

They deposited their piles of luggage in the ancient elevator. "I don't like this," Chude said. "Getting stuck in an elevator is my worst nightmare and this one looks risky." Creaking and groaning, the old rattletrap moved slowly upward and finally came to a bumpy, clanging halt on the fourth floor.

"Step two. How do we get into this place?" Eddie peered at Janet through the dim light with a questioning look. Chude jiggled the doorknob a couple of times and to their surprise, it opened.

"Looks like they left it unlocked, just for us," Janet said.

"Or maybe it just doesn't lock." Chude was having her doubts about the place.

"Welcome home, kids." Janet stepped boldly inside.

Despite tight quarters and the lack of comfortable furniture in their apartment, the first few weeks in Maputo were a delight for Janet. She had her children close by and in a safe place. Relishing the peace and quiet and the absence of overwhelming responsibilities, she slept late, took time to read during the day and wandered the streets when she felt like it.

The city had deteriorated during the war years. Buildings were in need of paint and repair. Some were crumbling, suffering from a decade of neglect. Most of the government officials—the Portuguese colonials—deserted their jobs and left within hours after independence was declared. Their departure left the administration of the new nation in shambles. In some cases, Portuguese nationals willfully destroyed buildings and machines, venting their anger at the demise of their elitist lifestyle.

After Janet scrubbed the grime from the apartment windows, she discovered a spectacular view of the bay. She looked forward to watching the sun disappear over the horizon each evening. She knew this was the sort of leisure she needed right now but true to her nature, before long she felt restored and ready to go to work. When weeks passed and she heard nothing about the role she was to have in the new government, she became restless. "I've been so busy for so long that these endless hours with nothing to do make me anxious."

"Cool it, Mom. You'll be busy again soon enough." Eddie had lived with his mother long enough to understand her need to be busy, to feel productive.

Janet hoped the position she'd be offered in the new government would be in foreign affairs, an area where she could put to use the skills she had developed while fundraising and seeking solidarity for the Mozambique Institute in so many countries. She was confident that her reputation with foreign governments had grown to a point where she could offer assistance to the newly forming, economically strapped Mozambique government. She had overcome her perceived youthful look and "cuteness" and earned genuine respect among her foreign benefactors. Samora knew it. Janet waited.

When she had a particularly knotty problem to solve, Janet had formed the habit of discussing it with Eduardo. *What would he have done?* she wondered. He remained a vivid, real force in her life. Checking in with him seemed the most natural thing in the world to her.

"I need a job," she told Eduardo one evening as she watched the sun go down. She sank back into the only easy chair in the apartment and lifted her glass of wine to him. "You know, Eduardo, everyone around here is busy, busy, busy getting this new government going. But not me. I have nothing to do. I think Frelimo and Samora have forgotten me. And just so you know it for certain, I have not forgotten you. I count on you as much as I ever did."

"Be patient. Give them time. Give yourself some time. They need you. There will be a place for you." Eduardo's booming voice echoed through the room, or was it just in her head? A single tear trickled down Janet's cheek.

Patience just does not suit me, she had to admit after giving Eduardo's wait-and-see suggestion a try. Waiting only made her more restless and discontent. Perhaps a visit to her family in the U.S. would give her a new perspective. She booked a flight.

"Have you thought about coming home for good now the war is over? Janet was not surprised when her mother asked. "You have so much knowledge and experience, you could get a great job in the State Department or maybe with a foundation."

Janet smiled. "My heart is in Mozambique, Mom. My family is there. I look white, but it is only skin deep. I'm one of them. Mozambique will always be my home. I want to live and work in my own country." When Janet returned to Maputo, she formalized those feelings by completing papers to apply for Mozambican citizenship.

Just when she had concluded that the Party no longer had any use for her services, she was offered a job as Director of Social Services for the new nation. It was not the position she'd hoped for, not one she was really trained to do, but it was a chance to go back to work. She accepted.

Party members had been searching for the right job for her for a long time. It had to be politically correct, Janet would come to understand, a position that would not have a negative effect on the independent image the new government was trying so hard to promote. At any cost, the black leaders were committed to avoiding the impression that they needed guidance, especially from anyone who was white. And the fact that she was a woman and an American did not work in her favor.

Working in foreign affairs would have made Janet too visible. Despite her sacrifices over many years to achieve freedom for Mozambique; regardless of her expertise the fact remained: Her skin color and her gender were all wrong. Nothing could change those things. Janet was forced to recognize that however black she felt inside, in this place she would always cast a long white shadow.

Janet and Samora had been friends since the early days of the liberation movement. She had housed and cared for Josina and accepted Samito into her family circle. But in this new era, politics and circumstances were interfering, causing an uncomfortable barrier to emerge between them.

Janet's awkward place in the Frelimo hierarchy was emphasized when a parade was planned to commemorate the eleventh anniversary of the beginning of the revolution. Samora felt an obligation to include Janet among the dignitaries on the stand reviewing the parade, in fact needed and wanted her to be there to represent Eduardo. But colleagues objected. She could not appear on the reviewing stand. It would not look right to have a white woman among the VIPs. In the end she was relegated to what Samora called "a position of honor" in a spot out of public view.

As she took up her new duties creating a department of social services, Janet revived. She directed all her energy to her job. A nagging question about how she was going to fit into the government structure remained as she began her work, but she put it aside with the knowledge that there was little she could do about it.

Under colonial rule, no attempt was made to provide for those in need of social services. That kind of assistance was viewed as the duty

of the private sector or the family. This policy meant that social assistance was haphazard if it occurred at all. Frelimo was committed to
providing services for everyone in need; children, old people and the
handicapped. *A tall order for a new nation dependent on financial aid
from other countries,* Janet mused.

She stayed loyal to Frelimo as she went about her work, but found
herself chafing at the Party's Marxist leanings. She was incredibly
bored by long-winded "cell" meetings that occurred more often than
she would have liked and didn't seem to get much accomplished.
She had a tendency to do things her own way, often refusing to tow a
socialistic line when it made no sense to her. She worried that changes
were being implemented too fast; that some of the things she was
being asked to do were just not feasible, especially in the rural areas
where people were slow to change their ways.

Yet, her job reignited her enthusiasm for problem solving. She attacked with vigor. "I'm not quite sure what I'm doing," she wrote to
her parents. "But then, all of us are struggling to bring this shaky new
government to life. We're flailing around in the same leaky boat, doing
our best to keep it afloat."

It was her relationship with Helder Martins, head of the ministry
of health that oversaw social services and was her boss that eventually
caused her to leave her job. Health issues were his concern; he had
little interest in social services and gave Janet only minimal support.
She struggled for months, frustrated by her boss's lack of interest in
what she was doing. Even so, she was able to lay the groundwork for
the policies and activities of the Social Affairs Department that exist
to this day. One day in 1978, as she sat waiting for Helder Martins in
his office to discuss with him the establishment of pre-schools, she
suddenly collapsed on his floor. Janet was hospitalized and prescribed
a long rest. "I have recognized a pattern I seem to have. Instead of
stopping and re-evaluating when things get really, really bad, I tend
to respond by continuing to work at a furious pace until I crash and
burn," she explained to Martins. She did not return to her job.

Chapter 26
New Love

After a time of recuperation, Janet accepted a new job. She was assigned to the Ministry of Planning as Director of International Cooperation. She became responsible for receiving delegations from abroad that came to Mozambique, tending to all the details surrounding their visits. She also worked with "cooperantes," people assigned to Mozambique from donor countries to provide technical assistance to the new nation. These experts were controversial because they were routinely paid much more than their Mozambican counterparts. The Mozambicans had less technical expertise but were more knowledgeable about what was likely to work best in their culture. This meant that there was some built-in conflict in her job, but she felt confident in handling it. This was a job she enjoyed.

After she had been on the job for several months, she was forced to take time off because of problems with her leg. She had suffered from a blood clot years ago in

Tanzania and it returned to incapacitate her at times. But it was a change in her personal life, not in the status of her health, that eventually caused her to leave her job.

She fell in love. "You can't imagine what it is like to come home every night to an empty house and to be greeted only by cats and dogs," she told a friend. She had been a widow for a decade by this time.

"I miss the interaction and companionship that occurs in a compatible marriage. I'm a social person. I need the back and forth of stimulating conversation." When Janet explained that she had met someone, her friend smiled. She had decided to marry.

*****

In 1979 Eduardo's mortal remains, along with those of other slain revolutionary heroes, were brought from Tanzania to Maputo and interred in Heroes Square. Janet spoke to a crowd gathered for the solemn ceremony. "I'm so happy that Eduardo is back home at long last. Now he is where he belongs." The people cheered.

The event was symbolic for Janet, signaling the closure of an era. Eduardo would always be very much alive for her, but now she was at peace. She was able to give herself permission to move on—to enrich her personal life.

A few days after the ceremony, she made an appointment to see President Samora Machel. She wasted no time with formalities. "I have fallen in love and I plan to marry. I hope you will understand and be happy for me." She paused and waited to see how he would react.

*****

Anuar Mussagy Ibrahim grew up in Manjacaze, the same remote village where Eduardo spent his childhood. Like Eduardo, he was orphaned when he was a young boy. He was apprenticed to a plumber at age 12. As a young man he served in the military. At the time of independence, worked at the National Bank in Quelimane, a seaport north of Maputo and capital of the province of Zambezia. He'd become a dedicated Frelimo Party member and was committed to nurturing the fledgling trade unions in Zambezia.

Janet approached him at a Frelimo meeting in 1977. She had a special interest in the establishment of trade unions and wanted to learn about the work he had been doing.

From trade union talk they moved on. "Sometimes the task of reshaping this country is like trying to budge a stubborn old elephant with your bare hands." Janet spoke directly, out of her own experience.

"Tell me about it. It's good to see change on the horizon, but waiting for it take shape is unbearably tiresome," he responded. They talked together for a long time.

When Anuar became Director of the People's Shops in Zambezia, he often came to Maputo on business. His friendship with Janet flourished. They met for dinner when he was in town. They took long walks together.

"Time flies when I spend it with you," Janet remarked. She was beginning to wonder if their friendship might develop into something more. While her feelings for Anuar lacked the passion of her early love, he offered her the comfort and the joy of a companion to relieve her loneliness. By 1979 they had made a commitment to each other.

*****

Samora smiled when he heard Janet's news. "I couldn't be happier for you. My blessings and good wishes." He gave her a hug. "I know Graça will be delighted."

"We're not in a hurry," We probably won't marry for a year or so."

"Good." he replied. "I'll ask Graça to help you with plans. She'll want to discuss all the details with you."

Samora and Graça met in Tanzania after Josina's death. They waited to marry until after independence, when they could have a ceremony in Maputo. As the course of history played out, Samora died under suspicious circumstances in 1986. Graça eventually married Nelson Mandela to become the only woman in history to be married to two heads of state.

Janet breathed a relieved sigh as she headed home, overjoyed and a little surprised by Samora's unhesitating acceptance of her decision. She'd been nervous about sharing her plans with him. She understood African tradition. A widow is the property of her husband's family. Frelimo claimed her as one of their own, the widow of their leader. She thought it likely that Party members would object loudly to her plan to marry, feeling that she had deserted them. To them, she was the living symbol of Frelimo founder Eduardo Mondlane, the nation's hero. Her marriage would risk that status and mean changing her name.

*****

Graça was visibly ill at ease when she paid Janet a visit a few months later. "So good to see you." Janet took her hand. "Let's have a cup of tea and put our feet up on the porch." Graça hesitated for a moment, as if she were in too much of a hurry to do that. But she seemed to have a change of heart and relaxed a little, seeking out a comfortable chair. Staring into her cup, she slowly stirred three lumps of sugar into her tea.

153

"Janet," she began, lifting her head to meet Janet's eyes. "Samora and I cannot come to your wedding."

"Has something important come up? Is there a problem?"

"Samora isn't sharing everything with me but I know he's facing a dilemma. His loyalty to you and his loyalty to the Party are in direct conflict. No one in the Permanent Political Committee approves of your marriage. They don't have the power to prevent it, but they have their ways of expressing disapproval."

"I'm not entirely surprised by this, you know."

"I might as well tell you. I'm furious with Samora for his change of heart. But I'm his wife and I must stay loyal to him. I reminded him that after Josina died, the Party encouraged him to remarry, even suggesting that he should do so before returning to Maputo. Party officials thought he would seem more dignified as a married man. Women are a whole different case."

Pressure from the Party was on. Janet was called to Party headquarters to meet with a group of men who she knew as friends and comrades during the war years. "You are our mother. We cannot allow you to marry. You have a responsibility to keep the Mondlane name unspoiled." Joaquim Chissano, who would one day secede Samora as president of the country, spoke for the group.

Janet listened as each of them expressed their objections. "You would no longer be Janet Mondlane." Another threatened that she would be forced to give up her home, provided to her by Frelimo. She remained silent and left the meeting too angry to respond to their objections.

Then her children were called to Party headquarters and the seriousness of the situation was explained to them. Every few days a Party member met with Janet to try to talk her out of marrying Anuar. Old criticisms arose such as the fact that she had refused to wear black and dressed her young daughters in pink for Eduardo's funeral. This had nothing to do with current circumstances but in the eyes of some was evidence of her refusal to abide by established tradition.

At one point, a Party member came to her house with a tape recorder to question her. She was humiliated and fell silent, refusing to answer his questions.

Eddie and Chude were quick to defend their mother. "It's about time you focus on your private life, Mom. You've done so much for the Party—sometimes too much." Chude looked her right in the eye.

"You're strong. Don't give in to them."

"Agreed." Eddie chimed in. "It's high time you moved on." Eddie and Chude knew all about "Party rules" from their time spent studying in Russia under a Communist regime. In Mozambique, they found themselves out of sync with the current culture and had a difficult time becoming enthusiastic supporters of the Frelimo spirit and ideology.

At first, Nyeleti, who had spent so much time with the Machel family, felt conflicted about her mother's plan to marry. She could sympathize with Samora's dilemma in a way her siblings could not. She knew he felt close to her mother. She also knew he had the guardians of African tradition to deal with when it came to putting his stamp of approval on Janet's plans to marry.

"Graça was so angry at Samora when he finally agreed with the Party and refused to sanction Janet's plans to marry," Nyeleti told her mother. "She was shouting at him about how unfair it was. He was pretty quiet, but he did not change his mind."

Janet confided in her own mother as she struggled for the second time in her life, with opposition from those closest to her to the man she wanted to marry. "I refuse to buckle under to the Central Committee, many who are men about my age, who have divorced to marry younger women without the least bit of criticism from the Party. My problem is that I am a woman and that I would bring a man into the circle, something unheard of here. That is compounded by the fact that I am the former wife, considered property, of the family of a great chief. My plan to marry would make me the property of another. In the last few years, I have become much more aware of my place in the world as a woman."

Fearing that she would appear too emotional, too angry, Janet had not responded to the members of the Central Committee when they confronted her. She took her time and thought through her response. She presented it to them in writing.

After independence I learned how it is to be a widow in a society where the female is dependent on the male for her status. A widow is seen as a social anomaly, incomplete, a threat to married women and a victim. I have been without the intimacy of a complete family circle and have suffered unspeakable loneliness for 12 years. Anuar is for me kindness and gentleness, the stimulation of conversation, the opportunity for 24-hour-a-day sharing that I have been without for so long.

Nothing can tarnish Eduardo Mondlane's place in the history of this country. I may be seen as his living representative now but he will be equally revered when I am gone. Nothing will ever change the place he holds in my heart. I know he would want me to find happiness.

If Frelimo gives their blessing and my remarriage is seen as a normal happening in a human being's life, the Mozambican people will want to share my happiness as well. I see the underlying problem here as the fact that I am a woman, a piece of property to be passed to the man's family upon marriage. The concept of woman as property must be attacked with the same revolutionary vigor as that which drives the class struggle. There is no time to be lost in the fight against this injustice to women.

When I wished to marry Eduardo, my family did not want to know him because he was black and from an unknown society. When I wished to marry Anuar, Samora, the representative of my Frelimo family, gave his blessing and that allowed me to hope that the other members of my Frelimo family would welcome my decision. I could say that it does not matter what my Frelimo family thinks, but it would be unbearable pain for me to be forced to choose between them and my marriage to Anuar.

My children understand that they need not say goodbye to their father in order to say hello to a new friend. No one will ever take Eduardo's place in their hearts, but they welcome the end to their mother's loneliness.

"You want me to renounce my name even though it has become an integral part of who I am. I was given it by the brilliant, intellectual man that I married who gave up his academic career to initiate a revolution by uniting the Mozambican people, declaring war on the Portu-

156

guese and in the end giving his life for the cause. Janet Rae Mondlane did not disappear when she became a widow. Instead I worked to support the liberated areas and during the first years of independence supported and defended Frelimo.

Before she signed her name, Janet reminded her comrades in the Party that they were all human beings and that loving human relationships, both individual and collective, are necessary to the process of social transformation.

Feeling depressed and broken, she boarded a plane to Geneva to spend some time in her place of refuge with her friend, Jean-Paul Widmer.

Libby James

158

Chapter 27
Rural Life

After a few days in Switzerland, Janet began to feel better. She walked for miles around Lake Geneva in the gentle autumn rain and visited with Jean-Paul, always a support for her. It felt good to be a long way away from Mozambique, far from angry confrontations with people who had been her colleagues; friends who had been as fervently committed as she was to the cause of independence. But sometimes the whole ugly scene in Maputo haunted her. She did her best to rid herself of a sense of betrayal and move forward.

"How much can they ask of me? How much must I give? I have every right to live a rich and full personal life regardless of my gender and in spite of outdated African family traditions." Jean-Paul listened and nodded.

"I'm so glad you came here. Being away will give you time to sort out your thoughts."

"You are good for me, Jean-Paul. You don't tell me what to do. Instead you give me time and space, just what I need."

By May, Janet's anger had lessened. She was ready to go home and move ahead with her new life, whatever it might bring.

*****

Janet and Anuar married in June 1981. The Mondlane children, the Machel children and Janet's loyal women friends attended the simple ceremony. Janet's women friends did not care about any consequences that might result from their attendance. Marcos Namashula, formerly Mozambique's ambassador to the United States, came and so did author Luis Bernardo Honwana and artist Nataniel Moiane, all of them out of loyalty to Janet. Anuar's two children were there, along with several of his friends.

A meeting of the Central Committee was called for the exact day and hour of the ceremony, giving officials a solid excuse for not showing up. A package containing a set of elegant crystal goblets arrived with a note of good wishes from Samora and Graça. Interesting, the bride mused. I'm glad that I don't have to live with the conflicting feelings they surely must be having about now.

Janet focused her attention on enjoying this day that would change her life, surrounded by people who cared about her. She directed her energy to welcoming Anuar wholeheartedly into her circle of family and friends. When the band struck up at the reception, Nyeleti approached Anuar and asked him to dance. Janet was touched.

"Mom, there's a whole new world opening up for you." Chude whispered the words as she gave Janet a hug.

"It's a time for rejoicing." Eddie smiled observing his mother's big smile as he swept her around the little dance floor.

Janet had found peace. She was reconciled to living with the disapproval of Frelimo and moving on with her life. Even at the height of her anger and frustration she could not find it in her heart to write off the Frelimo family she had been part of for so many years. She would never desert them but she could not imagine working for the Party ever again.

Janet was forced to officially drop her Mondlane surname. Now her identification card read Janet Rae Johnson, her maiden name, but the official change made no difference to anyone who knew her. No one stopped calling her Janet Mondlane. Anticipating that she would be asked to move out of the house Frelimo had provided for her, she and Anuar bought a home in Matola, a few miles west of Maputo.

During the time of their courtship, Janet and Anuar had talked casually about quitting their jobs and moving to a rural area where they could make a living by working on the land. At the time, their talk was no more than out-loud daydreaming, but now it seemed like it might be a good idea.

On a drive west from Maputo to Namaacha, near the Swasiland border, they came upon a country house surrounded by 15 acres of farmland that was for sale. They wandered around the land, kicking at the soil. They peeked through windows into the empty house. "It's a perfect spot. What if we, say, decided to grow bananas? We can rent out the Matola house and have it as a back-up to return to if things don't work out."

Anuar smiled. "It's definitely a possibility. I don't know much about farming, bananas or anything else, but I can learn." The thought of a whole new lifestyle was growing on him.

Janet was quick to make up her mind. They bought the property, collected essentials from the house in Matola and made the move. Then they set about figuring out how to live off the land. Janet pored over books about growing bananas. Over the years she had taken the dangling yellow fruit for granted—bananas grew everywhere--but she had never given much thought to what you needed to know to grow them.

There was plenty to learn. "Interesting. Bananas don't have a growing season. Listen to this, Anuar. 'Seedlings can be planted any time of the year. A plant takes nine months to produce a bunch of bananas and then it dies, leaving small sucker plants behind. A deep hole must be dug for each plant. Compost and fertilizer are critical and when the plants are small and they need to be watered every day.'"

"Sounds doable. I'm good at digging holes." Anuar's face lit up. "I like the idea of owning a banana plantation."

They plunged in with gusto. Janet ordered seedlings, dug holes and planted row after row of young plants. Anuar dragged hoses through the fields. Sometimes, when a hot wind blew all day, they returned to the fields in the evening to give the tiny plants a second drink.

The work was physically exhausting. "I don't know when I've been so tired at the end of the day, but it feels good," Janet said. "It's a pleasant kind of tired. It's such fun to see the tangible results of our efforts."

One day Anuar came home with a couple of baby goats. They turned the animals loose in the yard surrounding the house. Soon the grasses and weeds were under control. Before long they owned a small herd of goats that provided them with more milk than they could use.

"Maybe we need to learn how to make goat cheese." Janet set out to find a book that would tell her how to do that.

They fenced off a big garden plot and planted corn, squash, tomatoes, carrots and eggplant. They diversified their banana plantation by adding mango trees.

"What a joy it is to be self-employed." Janet took Anuar's hand in hers and gave him a peck on the cheek as he sunk into a cushy chair on the screened-in porch. "We're not living high, but there is no one to tell us what to do."

"Couldn't agree more." Anuar wiped the sweat from his brow with a grimy hand and relaxed into his chair. Janet handed him a cold beer.

Every so often, they welcomed visits from friends who had been part of their former lives. "Isn't it strange how friends line themselves up. There are those who will be loyal to me forever, whatever I decide to do, and others who cannot bring themselves to break away from tradition and the Party line. I can't spend time worrying about it, but I admit, sometimes it puzzles me." Janet looked up at Anuar, then bent to her task digging little ditches around the banana plants to make sure that they absorbed as much water as possible.

Janet and Anuar would likely have lived out their lives as farmers if an ugly civil war pitting the Frelimo government against Renamo, the Mozambican resistance movement, had not erupted in 1985. Backed by a white minority government in South Africa, guerilla rebels raged across the land, causing chaos and death wherever they went. Armed bandits raided the road between Namaacha and Maputo so often that Janet and Anuar were forced to join with a military convoy when they needed to make the trip into town.

Back in Matola, Janet was happy to see her children after a couple of months away. She shared her worries with them. "Invaders entered our neighbor's home one night and brutally murdered him. Other friends of ours, who own a pineapple plantation, were kidnapped by guerillas and held for ransom. It looks like we are going to have to leave the farm. It's just too dangerous to stay there."

In 1986, they reluctantly abandoned their farm and moved back into the city. Most of the businesses had been nationalized by this time.

Only a few private enterprises remained. Janet and Anuar needed a way to make a living. Because it was available, they bought a dry cleaning business in Maputo.

Janet was philosophical about it all, though she regretted leaving her quiet, rural lifestyle. "I'd forgotten how much I liked living in the country. It took me back to when I was very small," she told Anuar.

"The same for me," Anuar said. It made me remember the simplicity of my sheepherding days."

"We didn't know anything about raising crops, but we learned and we made a go of it. We can probably do the same with a dry cleaning business. Might as well make the best of it," Janet said explaining their move and purchase to Eddie. By this time, he was making his own way in the business world.

"Maybe." Anuar didn't share Janet's attitude. He soon learned that he could not thrive in the steamy atmosphere of the dry cleaning shop. "There has to be a better way to make a living," he told Janet after weeks of struggling with other people's dirty clothes. "Sitting behind a desk pushing papers is looking better to me all the time," he admitted. "You're right," Janet glanced up from sorting a huge pile of smelly pants. "There's just not much satisfaction in this business. The only part she enjoyed was the interactions she had with customers.

The war became more fierce and overwhelming and their customer base dwindled to the point where they found it impossible to make even a modest profit. None of the efforts they made to increase efficiency made a significant difference. People no longer had money to have their clothes dry cleaned or even laundered regularly. They had more to worry about than a clean, pressed shirt or pair of pants. As their income dwindled, there was less money to pay employees. Some became desperate enough to steal clothes from the shop and sell them on the street.

The same year that Janet and Anuar returned to Maputo, Samora Machel died when a plane bringing him home from a meeting in South Africa smashed into a mountainside killing everyone aboard. The South Africans who supported Mozambique's civil war were suspected, but the cause of the accident was never revealed with any degree of certainty. Janet went to console Graça as soon as she heard the news.

"I'm horrified and distressed, but not really surprised." Graça sobbed into Janet's shoulder as the two hugged, tears streaming down both their faces. "We live in a time and place where death so often seems just around the corner." Janet tried to offer a little comfort to her friend.

"I wish you the ability to keep Samora close in your heart. Talk to him, ask his advice, share memories with him. It helps. I promise."

"I hope I can be as strong as you have been for all these years. Thank you for coming to see me. Thank you for your strength and friendship." Like Janet, Graça had become a symbol--the widow of a national hero.

*****

Joaquim Chissano, Mozambique's newly installed president, hoped that enough time had passed. He approached Janet and wondered if she would be willing to take on the job of general secretary of the Red Cross for the country. "I'll have to give it some thought. Let me talk to Anuar," she said.

"What do you think about this offer from Joaquim?"

"The sooner we get out of the dry cleaning business, the better," he said. "How do you feel about taking the job?"

Despite her insistence that she would never work for the Frelimo government again, with Anuar's blessing and because she needed it, Janet accepted the job. She liked the idea that she'd be doing humanitarian work.

Working for the Red Cross was like old times for Janet. The work was related to some of the things she'd done as head of the Mozambican Institute. She made contacts with international organizations, something she was familiar with and did well. The Red Cross was overwhelmed by the results of wartime atrocities. Fundraising. Responding to disasters. Recruiting volunteers. Janet did it all. She came to have great appreciation for the volunteers. They had so little themselves but still turned when help was needed at the scene of disasters or in the office.

164

Always a woman with a mind of her own and quite certain that she knew the best way to get a job done, she wasn't without criticism for the way she ran the Red Cross. She had trouble understanding why the international office kept sending foreign workers to Mozambique. She insisted that Mozambicans were the best people to help their own countrymen. And they needed the work.

After considerable soul-searching, by 1989 she decided to move on. She met with Joaquim to explain. "It's taken me a long time to figure it out, but I now know that I am best at getting things started and functioning smoothly, then leaving day-to-day operations to someone else. When an enterprise is up and going, it is probably time for me to get out of the way."

"I want to thank you for your service." Joaquim rose from his chair and shook her hand. "Good luck. Whatever you decide to do, I know it will be done well."

*****

Anuar was about to take over a cashew factory near his childhood home in Manjacaze when the director of forestry for Mozambique approached him. He was looking for someone to operate a sawmill in Cuamba, a road and railway junction in Niassa Province in a backward area of the country near the Malawi border. Janet had just given up her Red Cross position, but she wasn't sure she wanted to make Cuamba her permanent home. "One busy hotel and a whole lot of bars," was how she described the town.

Anuar decided he could commute from Matola to Cuamba. They planned to have a small house in Cuamba where Janet would spend part of her time. Their house stood close to the sawmill and was reached from the road by crossing a narrow, soggy little path, an ideal breeding ground for mosquitos. Malaria was a constant concern in this place of high heat and humidity. Janet did her best to make their little house comfortable. She painted the moisture-damaged walls a soothing blue and enclosed the veranda circling the house with screens so that they could relax there away from flying insects.

When Anuar had to be away from the sawmill, Janet found herself in charge of the 20-man crew. In denim jeans and jacket, her high black boots covered with mud, thick grey hair flowing down her back and a white scarf protecting her mouth from flying sawdust, Janet watched over the frenzied activity.

A huge saw removed bark from a tree trunk and sliced it into planks to be measured, marked with chalk and cut into specified sizes. Janet took over during a time when there was pressure to fill a big order from a South African customer and get it shipped to its destination by train and boat before a looming deadline.

She made no claim to understanding the fine points of sawing up enormous tree trunks to specifications, but she had no problem observing that the process didn't run smoothly, that there were weak links in the chain that slowed progress. When the job was finally finished, she lost no time speaking with Anuar and suggesting efficiencies. "Maybe you should try measuring and marking the planks as they come off the saw that removes the bark. Move the saw that cuts the planks to size as close to the big saw as possible. You'll save steps and time and manpower that way."

Anuar smiled. "Why didn't I think of that?"

"Oh. And another thing. For safety's sake, get that blade sharpener away from the sawdust pile. It spits sparks all over the place."

"I think you'd better take over here," Anuar said.

"Just common sense," she replied.

*****

Back in Matola, Janet loved being around her small grandchildren who came and went often from her home. Twins, the third and fourth children of Eddie and his wife, had just been born in London. Otherwise, Eddie and his family would have been in Matola for the special family gathering they held every year on February 3, the date of Eduardo's death. The children and grandchildren all come together to honor the life of their father and grandfather. It had become a sacred time for whole the family; their way of keeping Eduardo's memory alive for the newest generation.

The occasion was to be a special one. Janet had plenty of time to prepare a feast and organize games for the children. She took special pains to think about what she would say to her expanding family to bring Eduardo's memory to life for them. And there would be time for her children to share their memories of their father and for the grand-children to ask questions.

Janet was happily retired at last. Or so she thought. But Frelimo wasn't finished with her quite yet.

Chapter 28
One More Job

An HIV/Aids epidemic had been devastating Mozambique since 1986 when a foreign traveler had unknowingly introduced the disease to a country torn apart by an escalating civil war. The disease spread rapidly and government efforts to curtail it suffered from underfunding, misunderstanding, and mismanagement. When Janet was asked to take over the floundering National AIDS Council in 2000, she said no. She was enjoying her home, her garden, her grand-children and the time she had at last to experiment in her kitchen. She became adept at making homemade ketchup. Life was good.

But Janet was still Janet and it wasn't long before she realized that she had been presented with yet another battle to fight. She reversed her decision. Then she went into combat mode.

Rejuvenating the HIV/AIDS council meant starting from the be-ginning. She researched the facts, including the beliefs and lifestyle activities that were influencing the spread of the disease. Only then did she wade into figuring out how to make changes.

She knew she needed to develop trust among the population, one community, often one person, at a time. So many people were con-vinced that AIDS was a punishment delivered by the gods and that there was nothing that could be done to control it. Janet set out to show them they were wrong.

She organized seminars to train AIDS workers to go out into the villages and towns to explain the facts. People needed to know how AIDS was transmitted. She set up clinics to provide AIDS testing and counseling. A campaign encouraging the use of condoms was launched with a series of explicit posters that went up wherever people gathered. A huge billboard in downtown Maputo pictured a couple strolling along under the protection of a condom in use as if it were an umbrella. Men and women were informed by word of mouth and through illustrated pamphlets about the importance of reducing the number of sex partners they had. Male circumcision was promoted as a protection against contracting AIDS and giving it to others.

Janet prepared a document with all the pertinent information she could find, to share with the media. Plays, radio and television broadcasts, and sex education classes promoted postponing sexual activity among young people. Peer educators were recruited for high school sex education classes and free male and female condoms were distributed in schools, at health units and in workplaces.

"We're doing our best to create a window of hope." Janet addressed a small army of AIDS co-workers. "This is a many-faceted war that will not be won with a single battle. It's going to take a long time, but it is not impossible."

During a rare quiet lunch with Graça at a favorite restaurant overlooking the ocean, Janet confided in her friend. "I've been at this AIDS job for almost three years and I think I'm ready to move on. The Council has a competent staff. We've launched lots of programs, and at last people seem to be responding to our efforts. There's a greater understanding of the disease and the ways in which it can be diagnosed, controlled and treated. It's time for me to go."

"Hooray for you! Do I dare ask if this might be the last in your endless string of jobs?"

"You may ask. The answer is yes. I intend to give all my energy to developing the Eduardo Mondlane Foundation. That should be more than enough to keep me out of trouble."

True to her word, three months later Janet turned in her resignation and left her AIDS Council job with a sense of satisfaction. The epidemic was far from conquered but the tools were in place to make it happen and Janet knew she'd played an important role in developing the organization into an entity capable of attacking the devastating epidemic.

With a clear conscience and a new rush of enthusiasm, she shifted her focus.

Afterword

T he Eduardo Mondlane Foundation became Janet's passion, her way to honor Eduardo's spirit and his work. She was determined to make sure that his dream, and hers, lived on in the world. She wanted future generations to understand the Mondlanes' political philosophy, struggles, hopes and dreams for the future of Mozambique.

She began talking to potential sponsors, planning organizational meetings and deciding projects the Foundation would undertake. The Foundation is housed on the campus of Eduardo Mondlane University in Maputo and within its walls is a small museum displaying mementoes from the liberation movement.

The Foundation has been active in sponsoring courses and seminars all over the world. Its mission is to address conflict resolution and peace and reconciliation, especially for countries that have been torn apart by civil war. Because of Janet's background and training in sociology, the Foundation is also involved with ongoing research in the social sciences.

In 2011 Janet received an honorary doctorate in education sciences from Eduardo Mondlane University for her work with the Foundation. She accepted the honor with these words.

"This is a proud moment in my life. I thank the university for giving it to me.

While I was working on my bachelor's degree at Northwestern University, I was doing various tasks for Eduardo to gain his masters and doctoral degrees at the same university. No computers, no wonderful software programs, no Excel with its formulas. Instead we used stiff paper cards with punched-in data (which we punched in ourselves) and rattling sorting machines. There were finger-numbing typewriters. I watched him sweat academic tears and I participated in the mind-breaking data gathering tasks for the doctorate thesis. As a result of this period in my academic life, I vowed I would never do a doctorate degree. I went on to do a masters in sociology but never was tempted to break that vow.

But now here I am, Doctor H.C. which I am particularly proud to receive, for this great Mozambican university bears Eduardo Mondlane's name! True, it has taken me a lifetime, with varied experiences in the armed struggle and nation building—but at least I have not written that terrifying academic dissertation! This university, like all other universities in Mozambique, strives to carry out its noble tasks in a country in development, where there are fields of poverty with a few pools of gold, where the struggle to survive is the priority, where higher education is a privilege. The luxury for its students to receive and afterwards not to give back to their people is not a choice for this institution. This university needs to give us the men and women that will take us out of poverty: to build roads, bridges, industries and great swaths of green fields that will feed us and our hungry neighbors on the continent. How do we educate more of ourselves, how do we cure our diseases, how do we maintain unity and equality in a world that seems to have gone mad with greed and division? A part of my dream for Mozambique came true, for since 1975 we can decide our destiny. The long road ahead will decide if Mozambique and its universities are worthy of the dream.

Not many people know that Eduardo's dream was that after finishing the task of national liberation, he wanted to have time in his life to teach at a university, to have the privilege to interact with students and Mozambique academicians and all the people of the country that he would see born. I enthusiastically shared this dream with him, and a part of it became reality in June 1975. On that wonderful day of 25th June, we won the right to decide our own future. My Eduardo is not here physically but our offspring Eduardo Jr., Chude and Nyeleti are here in this hall. I think without hesitation that the dream lives in every student of this university that wears the gown at the end of the course,

*with a diploma in hand. The long road that we have ahead is that we
will learn from our good actions and our errors. Today, young academics have the challenge to bring peace and stability to our corner of
the world. Tragically, in today's world, human security has lost its priority. In truth, our sovereignty exists in the will of each Mozambican to
embrace and defend the liberty that was won with pride in our legacy.*

*As I said, here I am standing in this one little space in Mozam-
bique, long ago having come from another little space thirteen and a
half thousand kilometers away in the United States.*

*When I was thinking about what I wanted to say in this ceremony, I
decided to speak about why I did what I did and not about what I did.
How did it happen? The story of each one of our lives is composed of
choices. Wendell Bell, my great friend, professor and important social
scientist wrote in his latest book: life courses (caminhos), both professional and personal, are often directed by unplanned experiences. At
crossroads, which path is followed and which hard choices are made
can change the direction of one's future. Totally unforeseen events can
shape individual lives. Despite our hopes and our plans for the future,
there is also serendipity, feedback, twists and turns, chance and cir-
cumstance, all of which, in turn, help shape the future, sometimes with
surprising results. Images of the future—dreams, visions or whatever
we call them—help to determine our actions, which, in turn, help
shape the future. The memories of these images linger and are often
used to judge the real outcomes of our lives.*

*From whence comes the motivation that guides life choices? I
clearly remember incidents from early childhood, like shelling fresh
green peas for my mother, pretending I was freeing slaves from their
prison cells; teaching my much younger brother how to fight the bully
who lived in our neighborhood. Childhood games turned into background scenarios for future work as an adult.*

*It is important to say that I had a religious upbringing. From the
age of five years old, Sunday School had an immeasurable influence
on my growth. Sitting on a little chair in my best Sunday clothes, I
was fascinated by the colored pictures of African boys and girls. The
teacher said we were all one people, under God. The years passed and*

as my mind developed, make-believe elements were diluted while the moral structure remained. The motivational framework stayed intact. As I entered teenage years, fascination turned to thoughtful contemplation of the world. I decided to make a difference in a corner of the world and go to Africa as a doctor. In 1951, I participated in a camp for young Christians, and there was a Mozambican lecturing there. There my direction in life changed. At age 17, I met Eduardo at the right place, at the right time. I had decided my future, and he entered it with unbelievable moral smoothness. And I entered his.

I had images of the future, images which were identical to those of Eduardo Mondlane, images he described in a letter to me in 1965, in the midst of the liberation struggle: "Our lives have got to be lived like this. We're part of history...helping shape a new world...a world which our forbears built up—both rightly and wrongly. Probably no one will notice what you or I have done and are doing, or the sum total of things being done in the present world as a whole. But I personally have no doubt that our actions will in some way influence the course of the history of at least the people of Mozambique, I hope to the good. This is about the only consolation that I have in compensation for my long separations from the most beloved people in my life."

One thought must be clear. What I accomplished in my life, I did not achieve alone. We were many. From 1962 until this present day, I say unashamedly that FRELIMO was my family; it encompassed, and encompasses, the comrades of my heart and mind. There were bitter moments. But the ties are bands of steel and cannot be broken.

Has my motivational structure changed from the time of the childish shelling of the green peas, of loathing bullies who fed upon the weak? The foundations remained the same but it left my imagination and found solid ground in the world around me.

The memories of these images of the future linger and they judge the real outcome of my life. Now I am 77 years old. My work is a long way from being completed. Since I am older than the majority of people in this hall, I take the liberty of extending a bit of advice: never underestimate yourself. If you want to change the world, you can.

One day I was lamenting with my friend Dr. Bell (by email) that whereas he had obtained great academic recognition and contributed to the intelligence of the universe, I had not done that and rather envied him his accomplishments. He replied, "Oh yes, I did, but you helped to liberate a people."

I accept this Honoris Causa with great humility. I thank the Eduardo Mondlane University for bestowing this honor. I share this recognition with my children who had to accept my decision, many times with enormous sacrifices for them. I also share this honor with my comrades of the struggle. In spite of the difficulties through which we lived, we knew how to bring victories that still live in the hearts of the Mozambican people.

*****

To this day, Janet Mondlane makes her home in Matola, not far from

Maputo, but she is a citizen of the world. She casts a long, strong shadow.

Acknowledgements

I would never have learned about the Mondlane story if I hadn't been invited to live in Mozambique with the Arndt family-- my daughter Jeni, her husband Channing and their three children. I am indebted to Janet Mondlane for sharing the Nadia Manghezi book with me. This story would not have come to life without the support and encouragement of my writing group, an encouraging editor and more than a few friends who have watched me bumble through the writing process.

About the Author

Freelance journalist, *lifestyle* magazine editor and staff reporter, Libby James has been writing for a long time. She's intensely curious about human beings, their quirks, enthusiasms and motivations.

Her credits include middle grade novels, *Running Mates* and *Frisbee Dreams* and *Wiggly Stories* and *Muffin Magic*, for younger readers. She blogs weekly at libjames.blogspot.com. While in Africa she blogged weekly at Come to Africa with Me. It was while researching the history of Mozambique that she learned of the story told in *White Shadow*.

She counteracts the effects of sitting and writing with standing up and running. She especially likes outrunning men in her age group.